LEVI'S ROGUES

ETERNAL TRIO

LEE SWIFT

KRIS COOK

Copyright © 2019

New content and revisions added to original content from Lillian's Rogue's
copyright © 2010

Cover Art: Petra Leitner

LEVI'S ROGUES

CHAPTER 1

Five years ago

THIRTEEN-YEAR OLD, Levi Dove grimaced when Aunt Grace clicked off the television.

"What was that for?" He folded his arms in defiance, glancing up at his aunt, who had assumed the role of his single parent long ago.

The hard-as-stone woman's blonde hair was tied back in a ponytail. She shook her head causing her long mane to swing back and forth. Her blue cotton dress was simple, though it might as well have been made of rigid iron.

Putting on her gloves, she said, "Time for your lessons, my boy."

"Now?" Levi could feel his frustration growing.

"Yes, now." She carefully retrieved the two books, one with black leather and the other with brown, from the large cabinet before placing them on the coffee table in front of him.

He exhaled his irritation in a long sigh. "But it's my favorite show, Auntie. Can't the lessons wait?"

"Record your program for later." She sent him a disarming slight smile, something that was rare from her. She had a tenacity that couldn't be ignored no matter how much a person tried.

Realizing it was useless to argue with her this time, Levi used the remote to set up the recording. "I hope the lesson won't take too long."

"It will only take as long as the effort you put in, young man." She nodded, clearly pleased with her win.

Levi didn't have any memory of his father or mother, as he'd been a baby when tragedy had struck.

"Let's get started," Aunt Grace stated flatly.

Levi didn't like the curriculum about all the creepy things in the world most people had no idea existed. He knew they were real—and important. Someday he would have to depend on this knowledge to stay alive. But sometimes...he just wanted to forget about his future and just be a normal teenager.

For years, Aunt Grace had bribed him with cookies to keep studying. It had been one of the few things she did that implied she really cared, though he never believed that. She was a woman dedicated to duty through and through. Like it or not, the absence of his parents had thrust him into her life. He was a burden, nothing more. If he ever were chosen, then he would be free of her.

Since Levi had turned thirteen, his aunt no longer used trickery or promises of sweets. Instead, she now demanded Levi take time to study or lose privileges. He missed the good old days. If he didn't pacify Aunt Grace tonight, he wouldn't be allowed to go to Michael's birthday sleepover next Saturday. Michael was a little older and had just been chosen to be one of the attendees for the high priest. God, Michael was so lucky. Being part of the high priest's entourage came with benefits—great benefits.

Resigned to his fate, Levi sighed and waited for the questions.

Aunt Grace opened the book with the black leather, her disgust for the manuscript evident on her face. "Tell me about this."

Levi knew the cursed pages so well that sometimes he dreamed about them. He'd never touched the book. She wouldn't allow it, which was just fine to him. This volume had been discovered at a hideout of one of the immortals the Conclave had trapped many years ago. Even being this close to it, Levi could feel the dark energy vibrating from its pages.

"Well?" his aunt asked, tapping her fingers on the coffee table.

He cleared his throat and then said, "The black tome is an atrocity called The Book of Timu. Though most of its words are ancient propaganda, there is information about immortals who live in secret around us that is useful for us."

Her eyebrows shot up. "Useful for 'us'?"

"I mean...useful for the Conclave," he corrected.

"Better. And what do you know about this book?" She pointed at the brown leather tome, her face revealing her warm feelings for this work.

"It's our most sacred text. Past members of the Conclave created secret spells to keep immortals from hurting us that are recorded in its pages."

His aunt smiled at him, encouraging him to continue. "And what else does it contain?"

He lightly touched its cover and could feel the warmth of the magic running through its pages. "It lists all the known *bloodliners* in the world. In ages past, some...high priests were able to...to..." He tried to bring up in his mind what she'd taught him about this book's history, but he couldn't.

She shook her head. "In ages past, the great high priests of the Conclave were able to use the book's magic to locate any living bloodliners, known or in hiding. Remember?"

"Yes," he answered, closing his eyes and continuing, "...to locate any living bloodliners known or in hiding. Unfortunately, that power has been lost for many years."

"True enough, but hopefully it will be restored one day." She sighed. "You're doing better than normal, but not good enough. You need to try harder."

As much as he longed for this torture to be over, he could tell she was just getting started.

Aunt Grace opened the black book up to a picture of a leathery-winged man with horns jutting out of his head and a spear in his hand. Black fire surrounded the image. "Levi, what kind of creature is this?"

"A demon." Malevolence all but leapt off the page. A shiver shot down his spine.

"That's right. And what do most people think about demons?"

"That they're evil and want to destroy humanity." Levi's frustration welled up. "I already know this stuff. Can't we do this later?"

She didn't respond to his protest, but tapped insistently at the page. "Do we believe demons want to destroy humanity?"

"Yes."

She turned the page to another drawing. "What kind of creature is this?"

He leaned forward and peered at the picture. A winged man flew with a sword in his hands. Blue rays of light shot out from him. "He's an angel."

"What do most people believe about angels?"

"That they're good."

"What do we believe?"

Levi rolled his eyes. He wanted to call Michael after the show so they could talk about the latest episode. If this lesson didn't end soon, it would be too late. "Angels, like all immortal creatures, are not to be trusted. They pose as beings of good will but are nothing more than tricksters."

Aunt Grace nodded and turned the page to a picture of a man who held daggers in his hands. Green smoke hid the lower half of his body. "What kind of immortal is this creature?"

"A jinn."

His aunt mocked, "Don't they grant wishes to humans?"

"No. They're evil like all immortals."

"Exactly." Aunt Grace turned to another page. "What about this creature?"

Levi looked down at the page. Similar to the jinn in many ways, but instead of daggers he carried a large hook in each hand and his smoke was purple. "That's an ifrit. Very nasty."

His aunt opened the book to two more pages, each with its own brand of immortal.

Levi trembled. The two immortals imprisoned in the secret chambers of the Conclave's Temple were just like the creatures in these pages. He'd never seen them, but he could imagine how terrifying they had to be. Most of his friends in middle school didn't know monsters were real. When Levi looked at these pictures, he wished that he didn't either.

Despite tapping the pages indicating her impatience, she said, "Take your time."

He didn't need time. "The one with the silver wings is a phantom. The other with the gray smoke is a shade. Both very creepy."

CHAPTER 2

9) BEFORE THE sun went below the horizon, the angel Rajiah was completely healed from his wounds from the earlier battle with the demons and ifrit. 10) He sipped the wine I had given him, and told me about other immortals roaming the earth. 10) Timu, you know about angels and jinn, demons and ifrit? 11) I answered him: I do. Everything you have spoken I have written down as you commanded. 12) He continued: There are other immortals in the world that side not with the Angels of The Alliance or the Demons of The Dark. They live in secret, away from the Eternal War. 13) Like angels and demons, phantoms can hide their wings. Like jinn and ifrit, shades can hide their smoke. 14) Timu, beware the Phantom and the Shade, known to humankind as The Rogues.

The Book of Timu: Verses 9 through 14—Chapter 3

Present

Levi looked at his reflection in the full-length mirror.

He wore a white linen high-collard shirt, which contrasted with his cropped dark riding coat and breeches tucked into his leather boots. His nineteenth century top hat and gloves were black. The entire outfit attempted to create an image of confidence and power, which he certainly didn't have.

He appeared as if he'd traveled back into the past to an age where formality and elegant dress and decorum were demanded, an era before fast food chains and Internet surfing.

If Aunt Grace had still been alive, he might have been filled with more than apprehension about this night. His aunt would have stood right beside him, her face full of pride for the good job she'd done in training him. But she was gone, killed on a hunt for immortals that had gone awry two years ago. Levi wished she were here with him now.

Tonight and all that entailed he would face on his own. He knew he was truly alone in this endeavor despite glancing at his four attendants, three boys and one girl.

The girl, the youngest of his four teenage attendants squeezed his hand. "Levi, you look so handsome." When the other teenagers' eyes widened in disbelief, she lowered her gaze. "I mean Your Grace looks so handsome."

"No need to be so formal with me, Rachel. It's just us in here, so for now let's keep things as casual as we can."

He spotted slight grins and nods from all four of his attendants.

Clearly more at ease, the oldest boy of the group stepped forward. He would be the next to take on the duty once Levi vacated his new role. "You really do look hand-some. Everyone will be impressed."

Levi didn't feel handsome, just frightened. "Thank you."

I can do this. I have to do this.

"Are you ready?" One of the others asked.

"I think I am." Levi scanned the mirror again. Nothing was out of place. "It's an important day."

The music in the other room grew louder, indicating the time had come.

"You'll need that." The youngest boy pointed to the ancient dagger still sheathed in its scabbard.

The weapon's wooden display cantilevered forward, appearing to defy gravity with its one-sided supports. The balance of the blade was an example of its deadly perfection.

Trepidation filled him at the magnitude of the new position he was about to take on.

Taking the weapon, Levi studied it. He'd only seen it once before, when his predecessor had assumed the role three years ago. The blade felt heavier than Levi had expected. The camel bone hilt was covered in symbols, and the scabbard had jewels and gold fittings. The steel of the blade showed no stains or nicks, though Levi knew it had been used time and again over the past several centuries.

The four attendants knelt before him. "Majesty, be well," they said in unison.

Levi sucked in a lungful of air, turned away from the mirror, and faced the large wooden door with the Conclave's rune etched into its surface.

Outside the walls of this temple was a metropolis with freeways, skyscrapers and millions of residents with no idea of the existence of evil immortals or of the Conclave.

A shiver ran up his spine accompanied by awkwardness and unease. The eldest boy, the next in line, tilted his head slightly.

They're waiting for me to speak the ritual words. "Rise. Walk with me and be my witnesses."

In unison, they responded, "Your Grace, we will, gladly."

Levi touched the rune, but it did not glow. Not yet. Soon. After. He swallowed hard, knowing what was to come. Then he opened the door to the chamber. He'd prepared for this moment his whole life, and now, like it or not, the time had come.

All the Conclave members, save him and his attendants, knelt in a circle around the mangled body of a man, the former high priest, Michael. Only four years older than Levi, Michael should've continued in the loftiest role of his kind. But he'd been killed last night.

Feandan, the head of the council, rose to his feet. The man was tall with dark beady eyes. Though Levi would be the titular leader of the Conclave once enthroned, Feandan would still hold the real power as the First. The man was a placeholder for high priest only as a formality for this ceremony. He would never have to face the monsters, though in every other facet of the Conclave he was in charge.

Feandan squared his shoulders, lifting his chin in a show of superiority. "Who dares challenge the high priest?"

Levi took a deep breath and then said, "I do, Levi Dove."

He stepped right in front of Feandan, pulling the dagger out from its scabbard. Then he knelt beside the body of someone who had once been his friend. Michael was dead.

With trembling hands, he lifted the knife over his head. The ancient traditions could be so demanding.

Levi had known for years this day would come, though it had arrived earlier than expected. Everyone seemed restless for him to continue the ceremony, to do what seemed to him so grotesque. But he wavered. Michael had been his best friend. How could he do such a thing, no matter the custom?

Feandan cleared his throat loudly, glaring at Levi with eyes full of disgust. The First wouldn't allow any more hesitation.

Levi clenched his jaw, and plunged the blade into Michael's dead chest. The crunching sound as the knife cut through ribs and flesh made him nauseous and dizzy. All new high priests sliced their predecessor's body with the dagger to signify the burden and the gravity of becoming the Conclave's high priest. Someday, he would lie on the ground with eyes empty of life as his successor cut into him.

Tonight was just the first step for Levi's future which he hoped would be longer than Michael's had been. What kind of future, no matter how short or long would it be? Michael had changed dramatically after becoming high priest. All indications of kindness and warmth vanished in the first few weeks he had ascended. Their friendship didn't end with any long discussion or disagreement. It just ended. Where once they'd been inseparable, Levi could count on one hand the times they'd spent together in the past few years.

Michael had been different in almost every way. Levi wondered if he too would be changed with his new role. He shook his head slightly to clear his thoughts. He still had to survive the next hour if he was to have a future. Another shiver of dread ran up and down his spine.

"The high priest is dead," Levi recited his line in a quiet tone.

The members of the Conclave rose to their feet. "The high priest is dead."

Another plunge of the blade. Levi dared not look. "The high priest is dead."

Since Michael's body had been prepared for the ceremony, the scent of citrus and roses filled the room.

Louder, those gathered in the room shouted, "The high priest is dead."

A final plunge. No blood seeped out from the piercing.

The smell, the sounds, the feel of that knife cutting flesh and bone, all of it invaded his body like a sickness. He breathed through his mouth and forced the bile back down. "It is done."

"Who shall ascend?" The crowd yelled.

All but Feandan fell to their knees. The man's dark eyes cut into him like a razor.

"I shall ascend," Levi said, glaring back at Feandan.

With a crooked smile, Feandan declared, "Levi Dove is our new high priest. All hail Levi."

Then, he too knelt.

In unison, everyone responded, "Hail Levi, holder of the dagger and tormentor of the abominations. Hail Levi. We live to serve you for the good of the Conclave, for the good of the world."

Feandan's knowing eyes glistened with anticipation, causing Levi's nausea to increase. Would Michael still be alive if the man had done more to keep him safe? Levi believed he would have.

"You have proven your worthiness, Your Grace." Feandan said, whose duty was to hunt immortals, leaving only two immortal prisoners alive at any time for the high priest. "The Conclave has acknowledged you. Will you stand by me?"

Levi's mind brought up an image of him using the two immortals in the dungeon below to perform his duty. He shuddered at the thought.

"I will." He forced the words out.

"Will you share the bed of our prisoners to ensure their power is our power?"

His heart skittered with fear. "I will."

"I, Feandan Darvis, Master Hunter and First of our order, acknowledge you, Levi Dove as high priest of the Conclave."

Still kneeling, the Conclave shouted, "Take him to the Rogues!"

He glanced at the giant doors that only he and Feandan would walk through. Dread filled every part of Levi. Distaste crowded in as Feandan led him to the cell where Michael had been murdered—and Levi would now be expected to surrender.

CHAPTER 3

17) I ASKED THE ANGEL, Rajiah: What sustains immortals? 18) The angel answered: All immortals must form a triad with a human to remain in the world. A triad of The Alliance has one angel, one jinn, and one human lover. 19) I asked: And the immortals of The Dark? How do they form a triad? 20) He answered: A triad of The Dark has one demon, one ifrit, and one human victim. 20) I pondered his words, then asked: And the Rogues? How do they form a triad? 21) Rajiah answered: A triad of the Rogues has one phantom, one shade, and one human. 22) I asked: Is the mortal of the triad a victim or a lover? 23) He answered: Only the Rogues know.

The Book of Timu: Verses 17 through 23—Chapter 7

Once again, Reno tried to pull the chains out of the wall, but they didn't budge. The new strength he felt should've broken almost any type of restraint. Not these. He wasn't sure why, and it only added to his list of unanswered questions about the craziness he'd experienced since his accident.

He studied the cell and its contents. There was a wooden table with an odd assortment of what appeared to be sex toys and lubricants. A rug with strange lettering and symbols that he couldn't read was hung from one of the walls. A small footstool sat next to the cell's only entry, a door of metal bars. Beyond the entry were two large wooden doors. Chained to another wall in the cell was a fellow prisoner.

His cellmate looked like immovable granite. At least six foot six inches tall. Short white hair. The guy appeared to be in his early-thirties, but probably not true since he was an immortal. Reno had no idea how he knew the guy was immortal, but he did. Actually it was more of a feeling than knowing. But what did he actually know about any of this insanity. Not much.

My life-after-death really sucks big time. Reno's ironic thought might've made him grin had things not gone from bad to worse of late. Especially after he died.

Moments ago, his wardens had moved him into this cell. *Bunch of assholes.* Still, it was better than the pitch black hole he'd left. And having someone dealing with the same BS made him feel less alone.

How long had they held him captive? He'd lost count of the days and nights in the windowless hole. It had to be at least a month. His memories were fading fast, but he did remember being a U.S. Marine. As he had in life, Reno refused to give up.

Unlike Reno's limited freedom in the hole, here they'd restrained him with manacles. The metal cuffs were connected to chains that went around a pulley on the ceiling then dropped to a ratchet with a handle on the floor.

The other immortal had similar bindings. Why? Reno didn't know, but he'd bet the screaming he'd heard last night had something to do with it. His jailers had been tough before. Now they were brutal. For hours, the humans had tortured him and the other immortal with wooden sticks that burned like branding irons but left no mark. Before leaving, they'd tightened the chains so his arms hung immobile above his head.

Reno sensed something big was about to happen that wouldn't be good for him. Somehow, some way, he had to get out of this mess. With the other prisoner chained up as well, Reno had no idea how, but with the other immortal's help there might be a chance. There had to be.

Reno wasn't sure how this supernatural stuff worked. Perhaps his cellmate had the answers he needed.

Hoping not to alarm their jailers, Reno whispered, "Buddy, how long have you been here?"

No answer. The guy didn't even look up.

"I'm Reno. Can't remember my last name. In fact, a lot of things are missing. Is that normal?"

Still, nothing.

"You're like me, right? Immortal?"

Gotta keep talking. Something will reach this guy. "The last thing I remember before I died was floating and spinning in a dark place. Some kind of accident, I think." Reno vaguely recalled that the cause of his death had something to do with an explosion in a Humvee in Iraq, though he couldn't recall any other details. "Hell, I can't remember. Anyway, I fell back to earth. Gray smoke surrounded my body, and then it disappeared. Can you explain that?"

The other immortal didn't move a muscle, but his chest rose and fell, so Reno knew he was breathing.

"Come on, buddy, I need answers. I only had a day

with…um…" Reno sighed. "I don't even know the name of the immortal who found me. Ninety minutes. That's all I had with him, my *welcome-to-your-new-immortal-life* mentor. The only thing I learned from him was I had been reborn. That's it. Then those fuckers attacked us, killing him and high jacking me. Come on, dude. What the hell is going on? Who are these assholes?"

"Until you've been here one hundred ninety-four years, shut the fuck up." The guy opened his eyes. His steel gray orbs revealed nothing. "Then, and only then, will I answer your idiotic questions."

Reno felt his jaw drop. "Holy crap, that's how long they've had you?"

The granite man didn't answer, but simply closed his eyes.

Not willing to give up, Reno tried another avenue. "What's your name?"

"You can call me *Mr. Fuck Off.*"

Reno couldn't help but grin. Despite the attitude, he had an instant liking for the guy. He had the demeanor of a Marine and might have been a soldier in his previous life. What battlefields had he seen? The War of 1812? The Revolutionary War? "Okay, Mr. Fuck Off, what can you tell me about these pricks?"

"Shut up." The immortal's hands curled into fists. "They're coming."

Reno heard a door open, then footsteps. What now? His body turned icy.

———

Jacques guarded his mind with a speck of his remaining silver energy.

Though he hated to deplete his resources, he didn't have a choice. The newborn shade, Reno, likely didn't know how to access his power. Too bad for the shade, but not for him. No one would get into his head. Ever again.

Last night's debacle had drained him. The previous shade had been foolish to venture an escape and had killed the high priest in the process, but Jacques had been foolish, too.

He didn't miss his tormentor any more than the others who had come before him. The man's delight in delivering torture disgusted him. Like the high priest, the former shade held no mercy in his heart. Any mercy Jacques had had before his capture all those years ago was long gone. *Good riddance to Michael.*

He'd never agreed to the previous shade's plan, but that didn't matter. The immortal had suffered for two decades and wanted to be free. The shade had taken advantage of Michael's inability to siphon off the energy quick enough to keep control. The former shade had built up enough power to break free of his restraints. Jacques had gotten some of the power, but not enough. The shade had communicated silently to Jacques that he wanted to take the high priest hostage and force the Conclave to let them go. That plan had backfired in a big way.

Instead of just stunning Michael, the stupid shade had killed him. Then the shade had made his last deadly mistake, grabbing the golden blade by the hilt. The shade's face twisted horrifically and his screams never stopped. Jacques had thought he knew the full power of the blade since he'd suffered its sharp edge innumerable times during his imprisonment. But he learned that its power was far beyond anything he'd ever imagined.

Just as the Conclave's hunter Feandan had entered the

dungeon, the shade had vanished before their eyes into the Ether, his screams silenced forever. The only sound had come from the blade hitting the floor.

Jacques had lunged for the weapon, longing for death —*for release.* But Feandan had been too fast, snatching up the blade before he could get it. The hunter was enraged, and Jacques thought he might get his sweet *lights-out* after all. But the bastard had stopped just short of driving the knife into his flesh.

Had it been mercy? No. Feandan saw him only as a *thing* to exploit for power.

Now, he and this new shade would face a new tormenter. There was no end to his torture. The shade was on his own, just like all the shades that had come before him.

The footsteps told him his eternal torture was about to continue. He knew the drill very well. He'd been through it time and again with the short-lived fuckers. Different faces, same assholes. He tried to brace himself for what was coming, though he knew it wouldn't help.

Feandan, the current bastard leader, came into view, followed by the new high priest. Through the steel bars, he stared at the man.

Wavy coffee-colored hair framed the new high priest's handsome face. The man's piercing blue eyes only added to his masculine beauty. To his shock, Jacques itched to touch him. His full lips looked delicious. Compelling. They demanded tasting. Transfixed by the man's wide-opened blue eyes and the seeming innocence in them, his hunger rose not just for satiation and power. *For him. Hunger for the high priest?* This wasn't fucking good, at all.

What kind of new spell has he cast on me?

Standing only a few feet away, the high priest lifted his

chin until he took on a regal pose, but the slight tremble of his hands revealed his fear. He obviously wanted all present, including him, to believe he was unafraid and ready. The man wore bravado fairly well, but Jacques sensed real courage underneath. That only added to his unexpected desire. He tried to quell his growing curiosity and rising need—*for him*—but the urge to drive deep inside the high priest erupted within Jacques like an unstoppable volcano. Nothing like this had ever happened to him before, and he reeled. In spite of that, to truly be with this tormentor, to really want him...that, he couldn't ever allow. This man, like the dead one, was his enemy.

"I am Levi Dove, your high priest." His voice sounded shaky, but the kindness in his tone only added to Jacques's overwhelming lust. "You will give me your power, and I will give you life."

His words were a cruel joke, at best.

The Conclave had learned well the perfect recipe to keep immortals alive to steal the magical power they craved without endangering themselves, allowing their prisoners just a tiny spark of energy before draining the rest of it. That was until the high priest known as Michael had made his fatal error with the dead shade. He doubted the bloodliners would make that mistake again.

Reno smiled at the new high priest. "Hey buddy, release me from these chains, and I'll do whatever you want."

The new shade didn't have any idea what was about to happen. A century ago, Jacques would've tried to help the guy out, but he no longer had the sanity for chitchat. Besides, the shade would vanish like all the others before him. Jacques had stopped trying to bond with other prisoners to avoid the pain of their inevitable demise.

Jacques wondered how and why he'd been able to survive so long when other immortals couldn't. At first, he'd held onto hope for escape, just like Reno. As that foolish sentiment decreased over the years, he began longing for the oblivion of the Ether. But it never came. He just lived on and on in this never-ending hell.

Feandan raised his hands and spheres of magical fire shot from his fingertips straight to Jacques's chest, filling his body with pulsing pain.

The familiar torture seared through skin, muscles, organs and bones. Agony, heat and throbbing consumed him, clouding his mind.

Struggling to keep clear headed, Jacques looked over at the shade. Pain and shock contorted the man's face, but he didn't cry out. That impressed him.

Feandan turned to the high priest. "Time to prepare the prisoners for you."

The two of them cautiously walked over to him and the shade, their nasty pain sticks positioned defensively. It was clear to Jacques that they were unsure of how safe they were. The death of the former high priest had rattled them and the rest of the Conclave. *Good...except they have no cause to worry.* After Feandan's spell, Jacques didn't have enough strength or energy left to hurt a kitten.

Without fanfare, Feandan stripped him and the shade of their clothes, and then prodded them onto their backs. Utilizing gears and pulleys on the chains connected to the metal cuffs on his wrists and ankles the bastard hoisted him aloft before swinging him down face up in a spread-eagle position on the cold stone floor.

He watched Feandan prod the shade into a standing position at his feet. The shade's ankle cuffs were secured to large metal rings bolted to the floor, his wrist cuffs attached to the ceiling so they dangled from the manacles. The new prisoner would be made to crouch all too soon. Once the high priest moved between them, he and Reno would be given just enough slack to move their hips. After all, what good would it do the Conclave if he and Reno couldn't doubly penetrate the high priest, the shade fucking his ass and Jacques fucking his mouth, so the high priest could steal their energy for his own use?

Fucking barbarians!

Once the high priest climaxed, the sexual ceremony would end. Neither he nor Reno would find an iota of real satisfaction. Crumbs. That was all they would get. Blips of energy. Nothing more.

Jacques suspected that once Reno understood his true role the Conclave had for him here, the newbie shade would become very testy. Perhaps the previous shade hadn't been stupid at all. Yes, the immortal's life was over, but at least Jacques's former cellmate was free of the Conclave.

As the new high priest drew closer, the handsome man shook and his blue eyes welled up with liquid.

Jacques craving for this man swelled inside him and he could feel his cock throbbing between his legs.

Hating the hunger he felt for the high priest, Jacques cursed.

CHAPTER 4

1) NOW BEHOLD, I, Timu, write, so that the truth of The Children of The Divine and The Children of The Damned may be known to those who seek. 2) It came to pass, at the time of harvest, that I, Timu, came upon a wounded angel in the midst of my field. 3) My wife and I welcomed the angel to our house. Showing mercy on the creature, we offered our best incense and balm, and the Divine showed mercy, and the angel was healed. 4) The angel told me his name was Rajiah, and He spoke unto me, saying: Listen! And I listened. 5) These are Rajiah's words, about the nations of man and the kingdoms of the Everlasting. 6) And the prophecy he imparted unto me.

The Book of Timu: Verses 1 through 6—Chapter 1

———

Levi had never seen either of the prisoners before, though he'd been part of the Conclave his entire life. Only those of the inner circle, the high priest and the First, were allowed access to the abominations.

The shade had just been captured only weeks ago, but the phantom had been imprisoned for more than a century, providing magical power for bloodliners. Levi hated the unfairness of the monsters living so long and yet his family died so young, especially Aunt Grace. For years he'd believed she didn't really care for him and saw him only as a burden. But after she'd fallen fatally ill from the wound she'd gotten from a demon during a hunt gone awry, Levi had learned the truth of her true feelings.

Levi had entered her bedroom expecting to find her unconscious as she'd been for over a week. Instead, he'd walked in and discovered Aunt Grace sitting up smiling.

"Come here, my boy," she'd said, patting the side of her bed with her hand.

He'd sat next to her and they'd talked for over an hour. She'd told him how proud she was of him, going into great detail of events he'd either forgotten or thought she'd discounted.

Then to his shock, she'd wrapped her arms around him. "Be true to yourself not matter what. Promise me."

"I promise, Aunt Grace. I will."

"Good. I'm tired. Better get a little sleep." Those were the last words she said to him. A few hours later she was gone.

"Levi, what are you waiting for?" Feandan asked harshly, bringing him back to the present.

Finding more courage than he really had, Levi shot back, "I'm the high priest, Feandan. I will take as much time as I need, understand?"

Feandan's eyes narrowed to slits, but he lowered his head. "Yes, Your Grace."

Pleased with Feandan's response, Levi glanced around the space.

The scene looked like a medieval dungeon. No cell phones or laptops here. His two unwilling lovers restrained by chains and stripped of all clothing, only added to the vision. He'd never seen such muscular bodies. Their desire for him evident by the lengthening of their massive —*Oh God!*

He knew the phantom's name was Jacques. His stare bore through him like a missile. What was the immortal thinking? Without Feandan's spell, the phantom could kill everyone present in a split-second.

The other immortal, the shade whose name he didn't know, seemed bewildered about what was happening. The oddest urge sprung up in him to tell the shade what was about to happen. *Very strange.* He shoved it down. Feandan would never agree to his stopping the ceremony for anything, especially something like that.

"The phantom and the shade are ready and under control." Feandan grasped his arm. "It's time for you to disrobe, Levi. No more stalling."

Levi had never cared for the bastard. His harshness and arrogance had always put him off. But tonight, Feandan was directing the show with him as the lead actor. All Levi had to do was say his lines, find his mark, disrobe, and...lose his virginity to immortal monsters. Anxiety squeezed him tight. The men he was about to clench with his ass and mouth would terrify even the most worldly man, let alone a virgin.

Feandan pulled him in close and whispered, "Make haste, Levi. Once done, we can join together."

He jerked free of his hold. "Don't. That's not happening."

Feandan shrugged, obviously not convinced.

Levi looked at the space between the naked immortals, the place meant for him. His stomach tightened.

Feandan extended his hand in a gesture of invitation to begin, but he knew it to be a silent command of *hurry-it-up*.

Levi didn't care what the bastard wanted. He wouldn't undress, not until he got a better look at the two immortals.

One step toward the phantom made him jumpy, both inside and out. Even with the years of treatment as a prisoner of the Conclave, the man's body looked like he worked out at a gym a minimum of four or five hours a day. Thick biceps, thighs, chest, eight-pack stomach. Jacques's photo should've been next to the definition of *ripped* in the dictionary. He guessed him to be at least six-six or more. A giant. *No, a monster.*

"You going to fuck with me or not?" Jacques's steel gray eyes narrowed, accusing.

The phantom's words were filled with ancient pain under the sarcasm. The manacles around his wrists and ankles looked heavy and had left scars. Every line of his warrior's body screamed pride, and yet he was restrained like the most dangerous animal. A seedling of sympathy for him lodged into a corner of Levi's heart. He tried to shove it aside and concentrate once more.

Levi had been taught to hate all the enemies of the Conclave. Aunt Grace had claimed the ancient writings in the Book of Timu were nothing but half-truths. But the sight before him looked so sad and somehow wrong. *How is this possible?* Against his will, his sympathy grew.

He saw a small lightning bolt fly over his shoulder into the center of Jacques's chest. The phantom's eyes closed tight, lids furrowing against the punishment and pain of the spell. The magical weapon had come from behind him. *From Feandan.*

Levi turned around to face the spell caster. "That wasn't necessary."

"Not your call, is it? Perhaps you should study the book a bit more." The corners the asshole's mouth turned up wickedly. "But take all the time you want. My duty is to make sure you are safe."

He'd disliked Feandan before, now he distrusted him. The creep hadn't hurled that spell at Jacques for his protection, but because he liked to cause pain. His enjoyment of the phantom's agony appeared on his face. And tonight was only the first night. Sex with Jacques and the other immortal would be repeated every time the Conclave needed power. That, too, was at Feandan's discretion. And how often had he caused the phantom unnecessary pain?

Levi considered asking Feandan how he'd failed to keep Michael safe, but didn't. No telling how the bastard would hurt the two immortals if he pissed him off more. "Please, I'll hurry it up. But let me get acclimated, okay?"

Feandan nodded, clearly delighted at his deference to him.

Asshole!

Levi turned to the shade. He looked up at the immortal, his chocolate brown eyes filled with confusion. If the chains weren't enchanted, he believed the man's massive muscles would've easily allowed him to break free of the restraints.

Levi took two steps up to inspect the other immortal and asked, "What's your name?"

"Reno. What's yours?" His accent sounded thick with southern charm.

The shade's chocolate brown eyes locked in on him like a laser. He couldn't look away. Reno's intense stare made him weak in the knees. Levi had the urge to run his fingers through the man's thick, brown hair.

All Reno needed was a cowboy hat and some tight jeans and he would be perfect, the perfect man. But he wasn't a man at all. Still, there was something about him that drew Levi. Why, he didn't know, but there was no denying the heat permeating his flesh. As it had been with the phantom, one glance and desire bubbled inside him.

"Are you ready now, Your Grace?" Feandan demanded. "Or should I subdue the beasts more?"

He couldn't bear him sending another torturous spell into these two. "Yes. I'm ready."

Trembling, he knelt at Jacques's feet, where Reno stood with his back now to him. He glanced at Jacques's hard, thick cock. His stomach went topsy-turvy. *It's now or never.*

Though still frightened, he guided his fingertips up Jacques's leg to his knee, but no further.

He turned to Reno. His intense stare made him shiver. Continuing to touch Jacques's knee with one hand, he grabbed Reno's calf with the other.

"Tonight, immortals, I take your power for the Conclave." He spoke the ancient words, then stood, backing away from Jacques and Reno. His legs felt like two cooked noodles.

Levi hesitated, trying to calm his anxiety before moving to the next phase of the ceremony. Then he slipped out of his clothes, folding them neatly. The air hit his skin, causing goose flesh to pop up everywhere, though it didn't have anything to do with the ambient temperature. He held his garments close to his body, surrendering to the urge to cover his naked frame from Feandan, and the two immortals, Jacques and Reno.

"Nice fucking body," Feandan said, moving his stare up and down Levi's frame.

Jacques's gray eyes darkened.

The phantom looked surprised at his modesty, which made no sense. How many virgins had stood in front of

Jacques before disrobing and then impaling themselves on his thick cock until he climaxed? In all those years, Jacques should've seen plenty of hesitation during the initiation ceremonies.

Reno's eyes betrayed the confusion brewing inside him. He had no idea what was about to happen. An urge to explain and beg him for forgiveness for what he was about to do rushed through Levi. *I'm losing it my first day on the job.*

"Leave us," he commanded Feandan.

Undaunted, the bastard approached him, wrapping his arm around his back.

Levi inched away, nearly stepping on Jacques while still clutching the clothing to his body.

"Don't be shy, my sweet boy." Feandan tugged at his garments, but Levi held them like a lifejacket.

The bastard smiled, trailing a finger over one of his exposed nipples. "What a shame that your first time will be with these two. I promise, when I come to your bed, I'll show you the pleasure a *real* man can give."

Jacques scowled. "You're untouched?"

Well, of course. The ritual demanded it. Levi frowned, "Haven't all high priests been?"

Jacques scoffed.

"Silence, phantom," Feandan commanded, then turned to him. "Finish the ceremony, Levi."

The asshole wouldn't like his next command, but he knew that climaxing under Feandan's impatient stare would be impossible. "I want you to leave. Now."

He shook his head. "Not happening."

"Am I high priest?"

"You are, but—"

"But nothing. If I am to reach an orgasm during this tripling, then you must go. Now."

Feandan didn't move. "It is not necessary for you to climax on your first attempt. There's plenty of time for that."

"But if I fail to reach orgasm and capture the immortals power in the next forty days and nights, I will be executed. That is Conclave law."

"You're getting a little ahead of things, Levi. There is time."

But Levi knew better. The bastard wouldn't hesitate to shove the blade into his chest should he not succeed in the allotted time. "I know, but I want to give it my best effort. Being alone will let me have a real chance."

"I've never thought of you as a risk taker." Feandan sneered. "Have you practiced climaxing by yourself?"

His cheeks burned. "I've done everything a man chosen for the high priest position is commanded to do. Now, please leave."

"My presence shouldn't be a factor for you if you've done the exercises."

Levi felt his face tighten with anger. "Feandan, you've no idea what it will take for me to orgasm."

"And you have no clue what these two monstrosities are capable of should you make a mistake."

Perhaps Feandan was correct, but the scene seemed safe since they were restrained so tightly. The bastard's presence wouldn't leave him a snowball's chance in hell of reaching the required orgasm to siphon the power from the two immortals.

Knowing Feandan was a sucker for praise, he said, "They look completely powerless because of your incredible magical skill. I'm sure I'll be safe."

Feandan grinned, letting Levi know he'd hit the mark with his false acclaim.

"If I need help, I'll call for you," he continued to placate. "Though I'm not Michael if I succeed, you and I—"

"—will complete the *Cavateerk*," Feandan interrupted, "the ceremony of union between the high priest and the First." The bastard cupped his ass, and though he hated his touch, Levi resisted the urge to pull away.

"Yes." Levi knew that sex with Feandan was required for the energy transfer, but he would deal with that disgusting hurdle later. Right now, he just wanted to be alone with the two immortals.

"I'll enjoy devouring your body." Feandan grinned wickedly and stepped back, removing his hand from Levi's body. "Alright, my sweet. As you wish."

"Thank you," Levi said, trying to keep his tone from exposing his utter revulsion for the creep.

"Treat him well or you know the consequences," Feandan hissed at the immortals, then left.

Levi looked over at Jacques and Reno, the strength of their massive bodies and their ready cocks. What would they feel like inside him, one inside his ass, the other in his mouth, rocking him to climax? His belly flipped again. He could feel heat shoot through his cock as his balls began to ache.

Time to begin the ceremony.

CHAPTER 5

I, Marcum, fifth high priest of The Conclave continue writing the history of our order, as those who came before me have done. These pages have been sealed by great magic to keep them from our enemies, the immortal abominations. The spells and rituals of our blessed bloodline can be found here. My hope is that generations to come will add to these, providing a great wealth of weapons for our kind. The pages also have been enchanted so that the reader may find any lost bloodliner, if they know how to unlock it.

The History of The Conclave and Journals of High Priests

▭

When Levi placed his clothes on the floor his naked body was in full view of the two immortals. His heartbeat ratcheted up, pulsing through his veins.

Reno's gaze held apprehension. "So, you're really a virgin."

Jacques shot Levi a jaded glance. "If you're not bluffing, you will be the first."

"That's impossible." Levi studied his face, looking for any sign of deception. "A high priest must come to his initiation ceremony pure."

"I know your cult's fucked up practices. I also know that you're the first to come to me untouched."

His comment blew Levi's mind. How could that be true? He'd heard the rumors about high priests secretly taking a lover before their ascension from Feandan. He'd always discounted the rumors as the bastard's feeble attempts to get him into his bed. Had Feandan been telling the truth?

Jacques mocked, "So, high priest, are you going to steal our energy or not?"

Levi gulped and knelt next to them. *Yes, I'm going to do this.* He touched their thick, semi-hard cocks to get the connection started and the power flowing.

Back and forth, one at a time, Levi touched the tips of their expanding dicks and uttered his first real spell. Its ancient words, if the caster spoke them correctly, would increase lust inside nearby immortals.

He could see the spell was working as he watched Jacques's eyes close and his manacled hands curl into fists.

Reno's breathing turned shallow. "Listen, sweetheart, this isn't they way you should experience your first—" The cowboy immortal's body went rigid as the spell took effect on him.

Holy hell! This can't be happening! Reno's thoughts entered his mind.

He jerked his hands back. *That's not possible.* There was nothing about this kind of thing in anything he'd learned about the ceremony. How was it possible for him to hear Reno's thoughts? Try as he might to remember any single passage that mentioned such a thing, he couldn't. Still, it was happening.

More of Reno's unspoken words shot through him.

What is happening to me, Reno thought loudly. *What the fuck is really going on? Pain and pleasure, but more pain. Fuck!*

Jacques's eyes opened, dark and accusing. "You're a natural at this, high priest. No wonder, since you come from a long line of fucking persecutors. You're hesitating. Are you struggling to finish what you came here to do?"

"N-No. I mean, yes." Levi touched Jacques's cock again, his mind whirling. "Stop trying to confuse me, phantom," he said, and then repeated the spell.

Jacques groaned against the magical pain, perspiration dotting his skin.

"I'm sorry," Levi said, hating every second of this. "I didn't mean to..."

"Sure you did," Jacques growled.

"No. It's Feandan who enjoys dishing out torture. Not me."

"Then why am I suffering from your magic curses?" The phantom shook his head in defiance. "Like I said— you're a natural."

If Levi had been standing, he would've fallen to the floor. How could he be so cruel? All of his studies hadn't prepared him for this. He closed his eyes, and thought of the mantras his aunt had made him memorize. He hated what he was doing.

Repeating one of them, he hoped to get his resolve back.

All immortals are evil. All immortals are evil. All immortals are evil. Over and over with his eyes closed he recited the phrase, hoping to relax his breathing even a little. But the words seemed hollow and false to him tonight. Jacques and Reno didn't seem like monsters.

Sure, Jacques was brooding and surly. Who wouldn't be after all he'd been through? But underneath Levi sensed strength and loyalty. There was a depth to the phantom that both frightened and excited him.

Reno was quite the opposite of Jacques. Unreserved. Open. Warm. What you saw was what you got. He was kind and charming. Levi could also sense that even after being captured by The Conclave, Reno held onto an overwhelming optimism.

Duty demanded he tell Feandan about hearing Reno's thoughts, but he wouldn't. The prick didn't need another reason to torment the poor cowboy more.

Why do I crave this man? Levi is my enemy, nothing else.

These thoughts weren't Reno's. They were deeper and full of ancient suffering. They came from Jacques.

Levi gasped.

Jacques's pain shouldn't matter to him. Levi hated knowing of it, almost feeling it, and most of all he hated that he'd caused it. He tried to close his mind off.

Had touching their dicks opened up their thoughts to him? His pleasure-pain spell seemed to be fading, as their lusty gazes freely moved up and down his naked body. He shivered. Could they hear his thoughts, too? *Please, no!* Their faces didn't show that they were eavesdropping on his mind, but could he really be sure?

He closed his eyes and sent, *Can you hear me, immortals?*

No response. He had to believe that meant they couldn't or he would explode into a million pieces.

The heat filling his body must've been from the gathering power. A shimmering silver light surrounded Jacques, and a grey smoke swirled around Reno—further evidence that the magical energy was expanding in the cell.

In the next few moments, he would lose his virginity when Jacques and Reno penetrated his body. The thought multiplied his nervousness. He doubted that he would reach orgasm tonight. Few records existed of any high priest reaching climax during his initiation ceremony. Likely, he'd need two or three more attempts before he succeeded. Then he would have to master siphoning their energy into him. That would come even later. Still, if a true transfer occurred, he was expected to provide them enough energy to sustain their existence, but not one speck more.

Unable to stop his hands trembling and too scared to care, Levi touched the men's cocks again. Thankfully, their thoughts didn't rush in. *If I can keep my head straight I can do this.*

Per longstanding instructions, he focused on the two immortals, his body, this moment and nothing else, willing himself to forget about Feandan and the others in the next room.

The world became still and quiet, but he was far from calm. Moving between the two immortals, he positioned his mouth next to Jacques's massive cock and his ass next to Reno's thick dick, but keeping them just a fraction of an inch away so as not to touch.

"Levi, I don't know what's going on, but this is nuts." Reno's chains rattled behind him.

Levi looked over his shoulder and saw Reno had enough slack to crouch to penetrate him, but no more.

"Tell him what you're about to do, high priest." Jacques's eyes mesmerized him.

Got to keep my mind in check. He closed his eyes and

recited the lessons Aunt Grace had taught him. But even as he silently repeated different mantras, doubt crept in. Reno seemed innocent. Jacques, though he'd likely participated in Michael's murder, had suffered more than anyone should—chained and abused for centuries. Wouldn't anyone fight back for freedom?

Levi whispered aloud, "We're going to...make love, all three of us."

Jacques scoffed. "What you're about to do has nothing to do with love."

He was right, but Levi had no choice but to move forward. Like it or not, there was no stopping this travesty. All his life he'd been trained for this very moment. He began stroking his own cock to expand the hunger he already felt for Jacques and Reno, hoping his need for them would drown out the guilt.

The two men watched his every move. As his cock stiffened, his body heated and electric shivers zinged over his skin. With his left hand, Levi reached back and gripped Reno's dense dick, and with his right, he stroked Jacques's colossal cock.

A crazy thought took hold of Levi. When the time came, what if he allowed Jacques and Reno to stay in his body long enough until he knew they'd been satisfied? That would be less cruel. But hadn't that been his predecessor's mistake?

A complete tripling with Jacques and Reno coming inside him would satiate them too much. Their energy would multiply, and the wrath they would deliver to the Conclave would be a total massacre.

Yes, there would be pleasure for Jacques and Reno, but no climax for them. Those were the ironclad rules. His safety depended on the step-by-step ancient protocols.

He glanced at Reno. The man's anticipation cut him like a knife. Did he believe that he would get to fill his ass in orgasmic bliss? Knowing he probably did crushed Levi.

Jacques knew better.

Later, the two prisoners could fist themselves, if they so desired. The Conclave and Feandan would allow nothing more. Now that he saw their slavery and their agony for himself, the cruelty of his new position felt like an anchor, sinking him to the bottom of a cold, dark ocean.

A mental picture from Jacques blasted him filling his mind, pulling him from his guilt. Jacques envisioned Levi *under* him—naked. His hold on him in the dream was commanding, absolute, as he kissed him deeply, controlling his body, his orgasms. Along with the images, Jacques's thoughts blasted into Levi. *I want him to submit everything to me. Insane, but God help me I do want him.*

The passion in Jacques's unspoken words made him dizzy with want. He ached with hunger and a regret he didn't understand...but couldn't deny. Tears welled up in his eyes. He cursed the day he'd been chosen for this role. But that didn't change anything. Conflicted or not, he was trusted to see this through. If he didn't, The Conclave would choose another to take his place. He would die, and *his* immortals would still suffer at another high priest's hands. This was his fate. Jacques knew the score. Reno would learn it. He had to keep moving forward. Like it or not, for the next several years the three of them would be locked collectively in this less-than-perfect dance.

Continuing the ritual, Levi leaned forward and kissed Jacques's nipples. He pressed his cock against Jacques's meaty dick. The feel of their dicks pressing against each other exhilarated him. Gooseflesh popped to life on his skin being so close to Jacques. *So close.* Jacques strained against his chains, but Levi stayed just close enough to remain safe.

I must have him! Jacques's face revealed his immense hunger, which only added to Levi's own lust.

"Crouch down, Reno. Touch me from behind." When Reno didn't move, he whispered a spell that he knew was painless yet held magical enticing words.

He listened to the chains rattle, and then he felt Reno's cock slide against his backside. He'd have to get the lube from the table soon.

His training had been specific about what was going to happen, but not on how it would make him feel. Anxiety and eagerness merged together inside him to create some new kind of emotion he couldn't clearly define or easily control.

Reno's thoughts slammed into him. *He's innocent in all this, that's clear. A virgin. Why is he doing this, Jacques?* "Sweetheart, let me help you. Unchain me and I'll—"

Reno, the high priest knows exactly what he's doing. Jacques's words exploded in the back of Levi's head.

He stiffened and froze in place. Can they hear each other's thoughts?

"How can that be?" Reno shot back to Jacques, making it clear that they could.

"High priest, do you have stage fright or something?" Jacques whispered, his hot breath warming his shoulders, and then he sent silently to Reno, *I can't endure another minute. Whatever spell he's put on me is driving me mad with desire. He needs to get on with this horror or by all that is holy I will break free of these chains and ravage him.*

The tone of Jacques's thoughts made him tremble, but he sensed that the misery of his isolation and suffering had driven any compassion out of him long ago. With the chains in place, he should be at ease touching Jacques's muscular, naked body, but he wasn't. And yet, he wanted to touch him, to feel him, and to plunge into the soul of Jacques. He doubted anyone could ever really reach Jacques that way.

Trying to sound brave, he stated, "No stage fright. Just easing into it. I'm the high priest. My pace, not yours." He hated saying that last part. Jacques seemed the type to give commands, not take them.

What kind of orders would Jacques give him if their roles were reversed? A vibration began inside him, rolling up into his belly and to the surface of his skin.

Once again, he pressed his cock against Jacques's dick.

Jacques's deep, strong thoughts rolled through him like a tsunami. *Fuck! That feels too good. I want him to inch down on me and clasp my dick deep inside that beautiful mouth.*

With Jacques's thoughts burning inside his mind, Levi's body sizzled with want. He pumped his own shaft and then gently squeezed Jacques's loaded balls with his other hand.

Jacques smiled. "Not bad, for a virgin." *Not bad? Fucking amazing.*

Pleased, Levi reached back and did the same to Reno's balls. The cowboy flinched only a bit. The two amazed him. In other circumstances away from here in the *real* world, he could imagine losing himself completely to them—no holding back. Still, he wanted to let go as far as he could.

Though he tried to keep his mind under control, he failed. Jacques and Reno's combined masculinity burned through him. He couldn't deny his own eagerness and lust for them. Before coming here, he wouldn't have believed it possible, but everything about them called to his overwhelming need.

My hard dick and constant shivers don't lie. But I'm

forbidden to think of Jacques and Reno as anything but objects, two means to a single end. Power.

Once again, he turned his head to catch sight of Reno, who was holding his breath, waiting for him with desire carved into his angled features. How he longed to turn over the reins to Reno and Jacques. They weren't virgins. He licked his lips, dreaming of what it would be like to have them in control of his body. If they weren't monsters, he would have surrendered fully to them. But they were monsters. Right?

Beads of perspiration dotted their muscular bodies. Levi tweaked his nipples, imagining the two prisoners' hands were touching him there. Everywhere. Despite the fact it could never happen, a delightful shiver ran up his spine and down again at the fantasy. He moved his hands down to his cock, squeezing and stroking his shaft and balls. His body heated to a roaring inferno. Though a virgin, he didn't lack any idea of what sex was. The exercises had prepared him. But knowing and participating were two different things.

Reno's thoughts entered him faster and clearer. *He's like a young handsome god. I've got to fuck him. I need to be inside him. Now!*

Jacques's thoughts were fewer and less clear. *Reno, pain comes next. Sex? No. Not really. Levi is very dangerous. More than any before. Suffering is all that is left us.*

The depth of his darkness terrified and wounded Levi. He considered stopping, but The Conclave would never tolerate failure to finish the ceremony. They'd secure the immortals' power with or without his acquiescence. The book mentioned one unwilling high priest that had been chained and beaten into submission. The cruelty of his peers, usually reserved for immortals, would turn on him if necessary.

Suddenly, Levi felt electricity dance over his skin. The room seemed to rock hypnotically back-and-forth. Energy amassed around the two males. He could see pulses of silver light shooting out of Jacques and gray smoke rushing from Reno.

Impulses, deep within him, hungered for more. Tonight's experience was so much more intense than masturbation.

He licked Jacques's dick, tasting the salty drop that slipped out of his tip's slit. He stood and took a step back from the two immortals—*his* immortals. They were fully erect, as was he.

Jacques craned his neck off the floor. "You think you're really ready for this, high priest?"

He wasn't, but nodded anyway. He walked to the table that had all the sexual devices, which weren't necessary tonight, and took one of the bottles of lubricant. He squeezed a healthy amount into his palm.

He applied the stuff to his ass ring generously. Now, he had no more reasons to delay. *Oh God!*

He returned to Jacques and Reno. He squirted more liquid in his palm, and slicked up Reno's cock with long, slow strokes. His moans that followed pleased him. Next, he placed the bottle by Jacques's feet.

I need to be inside his mouth, if only for a moment. Jacques's words rolled through him.

He and Reno wanted him, and he wanted them. His hands trembled, but he didn't care. He wanted, craved, thirsted, and had to have them inside him. Not for The Conclave or for the power, but to satisfy his needs and to know what it meant to be consumed.

He had to trust the enchanted chains holding Jacques and Reno, but as he worked his way back in between them, his anxiety blossomed to full-bloom. The immortals rock-solid bodies hemmed him in, but only the heavy breathing and hard cocks revealed the titanic craving caged inside them.

Levi could feel Reno crouch into position behind him and Jacques thrust up off the floor.

He could feel both their cocks pressing against him, Reno's against his ass cheeks and Jacques's against his lips.

A touch of panic twirled in his belly. The time had come.

"Sweetheart, just let me have one hand free," Reno said. "You shouldn't have to pleasure yourself. I can help you enjoy this."

"No. I can't." Using his hands, Levi guided the tips of each of their dicks to his entrances. *This is too much to ask of me.* "I'm really scared," he confessed. "I don't want to hurt either of you, but I don't want you to hurt me."

"You really mean that." Jacques's frown reflected his surprise. *What kind of high priest is this man?*

Certainly he couldn't be the only high priest to show any fear or sympathy. "I do mean it."

"Then let us come inside you," Jacques said.

Levi choked back sudden tears. "It's forbidden."

"Shh. I know, but there's another way."

"Stop talking. You're trying to trick me. It's all in the book."

Jacques's gaze never faltered from him. "No. You're the first to ever show any compassion or remorse. I never expected anyone like you to come to this cell."

"What do you mean it's forbidden for us to come inside him?" Reno's frustrated tone undid him.

In his head, he knew he wouldn't die because he with-held their climaxes, but the thought of not connecting with them somehow completely disarmed him. Tears rolled down his cheeks.

"That's how it works, shade. He's troubled by it, but he's still a member of The Conclave. We can't expect anything else from him."

"I'm not like them. Really, I'm not."

"We'll see, high priest." Jacques closed his eyes. "Do what you came to do, and be done with it. I want to feel your mouth around my dick, climax or not."

Levi's bloodliner passion would not be quelled. He'd saved himself for this very moment. The time had finally come. Their dicks knocking at his ass and mouth sent sparks dancing up and down his arms and legs.

Reno's thought drifted into him. *I've never wanted anyone more than Levi. Ever.*

Me either, shade. Jacques shot back. *Me either.*

Their joint confessions dissolved all resistance inside him. He took a deep breath and rocked his hips back impaling his ass onto Reno's cock. The intrusion ripped him apart. The strain and discomfort jolted him.

"Oh God," he whimpered.

"It's okay, sweetheart," Reno said softly. "Just breathe."

"He's right, Levi," Jacques said in a gentle tone. "Give it a minute. It will feel much better, babe."

Babe? Sweetheart? Damn their tenderness. It was undoing him completely. Fresh tears fell. It shouldn't be like this—so impersonal—his taking but not giving.

"I can't do this," he said.

"You must, Levi," Jacques responded. "You only have forty days but you have to get past this first before you can move on to siphoning our energy. If you don't, you and I both know what happens."

Was Jacques trying to help him?

"I know."

"You took way too much of Reno," Jacques continued. "Try again."

Reno's soft tone also calmed Levi. "This time, just take me really slow, okay?"

"Okay. I'll try." Again, he spread his cheeks.

The pain returned as Reno's dick slipped past the ring. He back into Reno taking more and more of him, but slowly this time as instructed..

Levi had never felt so filled. Every inch of him seemed utterly stretched.

Gradually, the pain eased, and in its stead something new took its place. What? Bliss. Want. Hunger. Rapture. And more.

Shameless desire took control of everything inside him. Unable to hold back, Levi swallowed Jacques until he stuffed his entire dick inside his mouth and began rocking back and forth taking Reno's cock into his ass.

Jacques closed his gray eyes and hissed his pleasure. He could feel Jacques down his throat and Reno inside his ass. Bit by bit, he got into a rhythm that matched his two immortals. The heat inside him continued to ramp up to a blistering boil. He felt ravenous for more. He'd never imagined it would be like this.

Jacques growled, "My God, babe, you surprise me."

There that word was again. *Babe.* He loved hearing that from Jacques. Loved hearing *sweetheart* from Reno. Loved every heartbeat of this infinite moment.

Levi could see his own red energy spreading out, as well as Jacques's silver light growing brighter and Reno's gray smoke thickening. No time to wait for his body to fully sync-up with the pain and pleasure of the penetration as he continued taking Reno into his backside and Jacques into his mouth. The time was close. Very close.

Christ, he's amazing! Jacques's thought pushed past his fear.

Speaking the magic words, he unlocked one of Reno's wrist cuffs.

"What the hell?" Reno said.

He released Jacques's cock from his mouth and looked at Reno over his shoulder. "Feandan would kill me for less, but you promised to help me and not hurt me. I hope you meant it."

"I meant it, sweetheart. I swear." Without hesitation, Reno reached around him and squeezed his cock.

"Oh yes. Feels so good." He risked a glance at Jacques.

Shock spread across the immortal's face, but before he could say a word, Levi swallowed him whole again and shifted his hips to take more of Reno into his body.

Reno feathered his lips across the back of his neck, which only made him more insane with lust.

The chains are too loose. Levi knew he should be worried, but he wasn't. He was lost to the electricity his two immortals were giving him. Lost and loving it.

More heat than before rolled through him. "That feels so good."

"High priest, we're out of time. You know Feandan won't wait much longer." Jacques's demeanor seemed wracked by confusion. "You must finish the ceremony and place the shackle back on Reno before the bastard returns or you will be in real danger."

Did this presumed monster really care about him? Jacques was right. He shouldn't talk to them, much less confide, but they shared this experience and he had no one else to trust. "I'm not supposed to let you come, but I can't help myself. I can't."

"It's okay, sweetheart." Reno stroked Levi's cock up and down, which felt incredible. "Just breathe deep and let yourself go. This is your first time. I want you to never forget it."

Levi took in a long breath, and then exhaled. "It's impossible to forget this."

Jacques growled, "Shade, grab Levi's thigh with your hand to take him even deeper."

"This ain't my first rodeo, partner. I know what to do." Despite his bravado, Reno complied, lifting Levi's leg. "I can take it from here."

"Fuck. That feels amazing." Levi heard his own voice shake. He loved feeling Reno's hand on his thigh as the cowboy's dick drove even deeper inside him.

Reno kissed the back of his neck again. "Push into me, baby."

He shifted back, and pressed, taking his dick deeper into his ass. He closed his eyes and bit his lip.

"Reno, he must take us both at the same time. Feandan will know if he doesn't."

Everything inside him light up like a thousand rockets launching into space.

They slipped into him like they belonged there. He shimmied back and forth on their dicks.

Faster. Faster. Faster.

His body tightened, and tightened, and tightened and then he went over the edge, shooting his load onto Jacques legs.

This is an orgasm! God, yes!

Levi sensed the two men were about to come, too. *Please, let them! Just this once.*

Feandan's voice cut through his delicious dizziness. "Enough!"

The bastard jerked Levi from between Jacques and Reno.

Exhausted from his climax, Levi slumped to the ground, but he could feel the power of his two immortals swirling inside him. Real power. A victory for him, the new high priest, but at what price? He glanced at Reno, then Jacques. The agony on their faces hurt him to his core.

"Did you succeed in siphoning power from these abominations?" Feandan asked.

If the creep had power to spare, he could've seen for himself, but he was low due to the spells he'd cast for this ceremony to subdue Jacques and Reno.

Levi couldn't let Feandan know that he'd fully succeeded. Not now. He couldn't bear letting the bastard touch him. So, he lied. "I didn't succeed tonight."

Feandan glowered at him. "How did the shade get his hand free?"

He opened his mouth to confess, but Jacques spoke first. "Immortals have more tricks than you know, Feandan."

The high priest sent a bolt of energy into Jacques's chest, proving he had a least a little more reserved power.

Jacques's body convulsed as he grimaced in agony from the pain magic.

Levi's heart burst in two.

Jacques? Jacques? Are you okay, buddy? He listened to Reno's thought.

I'll be fine.

Reno continued, *Tell me what happens next?*

The two immortals' minds were ablaze with anger and hunger. Clearly, they didn't know he could hear their thoughts, or they wouldn't have silently conversed with each other.

Jacques sent, *There's nothing next.*

So this is hell? Reno's thought buzzed like a wasp's nest.

Yes. Jacques's final thought was accompanied by a far-reaching anguish.

Levi's heart submerged to a dark, cold, and lonely corner deep inside him he'd not known existed.

Jacques and Reno were right.

This *was* hell...for him, too.

CHAPTER 6

IMMORTALS NEED HUMANS for life essence. That requires a triad. Think of the laws governing electricity and its flow between positive, negative, and conduit. The same is how the energy is created and transferred. Two immortals and one human create this transaction of force. It is called a tripling. We now understand why our ceremonies work to keep the power from the immortal abominations. If the conduit is removed after the energy is created but before it can transfer, the power remains with the human.

The History of the Conclave and Journals of High Priests

——

"You've come a long way from thirty-two nights ago when you first became our high priest." Feandan's false praise sickened Levi.

The narcissistic bastard could go fuck himself for all he cared, but he just nodded and smiled.

Has it only been thirty-two nights since the initiation

ceremony? He was not the same man that he'd been that night.

Feandan sat across from him in a throne-sized wingback chair, twirling his brandy in the crystal glass.

Levi sipped his Earl Grey, hoping to appear calm, though a tempest swirled in his head.

"How are your studies, high priest?" Feandan meant with the Book of Timu, of course.

Levi hadn't brought it out of his new chambers for this meeting as the bastard clearly wanted. The spell he'd surrounded the tome with made it invisible to all but him. Just to make sure it remained safe, Levi had hid it under the loose floorboards under his bed.

Feandan wanted the book back under his thumb, but thankfully tradition gave Levi the right to keep it as long as he deemed necessary.

As a vital part of his plan, he deemed it *very* necessary.

"Still lots to learn," he lied to Feandan. "Perhaps I'm just a slow learner."

One of the creep's eyebrows cocked. "I know better. Time is almost up, my sweet. Eight more days."

"I know." Levi set down his cup of tea. "Forty days since my accession."

"Correct. You either siphon energy, or you know what will happen to you."

"Yes, I know." The law was clear. Any high priest unable to produce the much-needed energy from the immortals within forty days would be replaced, and there was only one way a high priest was replaced. The blade. "I will succeed. I promise."

Feandan's angry stare unnerved him. "What are you up to, Levi?"

"What do you mean?" *Does he know? No.* If he did, Levi would be dead already. Or worse.

Feandan downed his liquor in a single gulp then said, "The last few of your attempts to gather power from the two abominations troubled me."

His heart leapt to his throat. "How so?"

"You keep asking for more time alone with them, claiming that it will help you with your duties, but you never are able to siphon power.

"I'm trying," Levi said, hoping to sound convincing. "Next time, I will not fail. I know what I have to do."

"You keep saying that. You seem *sympathetic* to the creatures."

He does know. He's just toying with me.

The last several weeks had been pure hell. Yes, he'd loved touching Reno and Jacques, listening to their thoughts about desiring him, feeling them inside his body. Even though he knew how to get around Feandan's new enchantments on the chains, he didn't release Reno's hand despite how much he longed to free him. If he had given into all his desire to feel Jacques and Reno's touches and released them, Feandan would have found out and his plan would have been derailed. No doubt Feandan wouldn't have allowed him to be alone with Reno and Jacques again.

Although a repeat of freeing Reno's hand had never happened again, Levi's climaxes had come like clockwork, each more intense than the previous. Reno and Jacques were denied release into his body.

The pain they endured from the rituals had stockpiled his guilt into something he couldn't bear any longer.

Reno's constant words of compassion had amazed him. "Levi, this isn't your fault."

But he knew better. So did Jacques. During their last

ceremony, he'd tried to pull the brooding phantom out of his dark mood. His mind brought up the images of that very night.

Levi grazed Jacques's lips. His eyes opened and he sent his velvet tongue into his mouth, sweeping inside until his mind exploded. God, Jacques knew how to kiss a man.

As their kiss deepened, he felt the phantom's cock thicken against his body.

When their kiss ended, Jacques growled, "I want to taste you, high priest."

Adrenaline flooded his veins. Like every night when he came to this room, Jacques's body was chained in the spread-eagle fashion on the floor. He crawled up his body until his cock touched Jacques's lips. Instantly, Jacques ran his tongue over the tip of his dick, dispensing an assault that over-whelmed. Even in chains, Jacques tempted him, warmed him up, and made him feel wonderful.

"Levi, I can tell that you like that," Reno said. "But the asshole will be back in here soon."

Jacques stopped licking his cock. "He's right. Best to get to what you're here for, high priest."

The sharpness of the phantom's tone stung him. "I can tell them we need more time." He stood.

"Don't bother, high priest." Jacques's darkness nearly suffocated him.

"But we can have more time together," Levi said.

"Really? I know your laws." Jacques shook his head. "Forty days is all you have to siphon energy and provide it to the high priest. You'll be fucking that bastard soon enough."

Tears poured from Levi's eyes. He lay down next to

Jacques, touching his shoulder. "I don't know what else to do. If could I would."

Jacques sighed. "I should have never let it get this far with you."

"Please, don't say that," Levi said.

"Jacques, just stop. We're all trapped in this hell," Reno added.

Jacques's unblinking gray eyes locked on Levi. "Do you enjoy torturing me, high priest?"

He rolled away from Jacques, curling into a ball, sobbing uncontrollably. Everything he'd said was true. Guilt consumed every fiber of his being.

"What's with you, Jacques?" Reno asked.

His gaze never left him. "I'm done. No more fooling myself into believing this is more than it is. We are his prisoners, Reno. That's all. Nothing more."

As Feandan refilled his own drink, Levi tried to shake off the painful memory but couldn't.

When Feandan and the attendants had rushed to find him curled on the floor in tears, they had taken him away. Even with only a few days left before he would be replaced if he failed, the Conclave's council had granted his request for a couple days of rest. Levi figured they didn't have any faith left in him to succeed. He'd used the time to form his plan.

"You are *sympathetic* to the creatures, aren't you?" Feandan repeated, which caused the memory of the other night to fade into the background of his mind.

"Not true," he lied. "You know that my work is taxing. Even the book attests to that."

He thought about bringing his new power to the forefront, just in case the brute tried to force himself on him. But Feandan didn't make a move toward him. Could the man sense the massive energy inside him? Impossible. Feandan's remaining power he'd received from Michael was long gone. Levi's deception about not being able to siphon energy from his immortals remained in tact.

"Just don't forget who you are," Feandan said.

"Never. I am the high priest of the Conclave. The two creatures are nothing to me, only power for my family."

"And for me, my sweet." Feandan smiled wickedly. "Let me show you around the bedroom. It will help with your next ceremony."

"The book says otherwise, Feandan. You'll have me soon enough."

"Or the blade will."

This discussion proved to Levi that he must act now if his plan had any chance of success. Time was up. Though he wanted to memorize more spells, what he'd learned from the book would have to suffice.

Jacques woke. Someone was outside the bars of the cell. A man.

Levi.

Alone.

Where were the guards?

He feigned sleep and suspected Reno was actually asleep. The chains that held him were loose, allowing him movement in the cell. The attendants only tightened them when their power-stealing ceremony was conducted. It had been several days since he'd seen Levi and felt his skin pressing against his body. He wasn't chained and spread-eagle on the floor now, and if Levi stepped close enough he could grab him through the bars.

Levi softly said, "I know you're awake, Jacques."

He didn't move. *He can't know I'm awake.*

"But I do know," Levi said, adding, "and Reno's awake, too."

Jacques opened his eyes. *Levi can read my mind?*

The shade responded, "Yes, I am awake. What are you doing here?"

"I'm springing you. And *yes*, I can hear your thoughts, Jacques—yours and Reno's. Can't you hear mine?"

"Sometimes," He lied. He'd never known any mortal, bloodliner or not, with such power. He'd believed that to be only an immortal skill and only with other immortals. Strange. Now he knew better. With more power, he would've guarded his mind from Levi and any other Conclave eavesdroppers. But he didn't have more power since Levi had drained him dry.

"I can't read your mind," Reno offered Levi. "Jacques and I do communicate silently sometimes."

Jacques curled his hands into fists. *Shut up, fool!*

"He's no fool, Jacques," Levi said. "And I'm sorry about what we've done to you—what I've done to you."

Sorry? I very much doubt that.

"It's true. I am sorry. Really."

Jacques realized Levi must've been reading his mind and the shade's since the first day. How? He'd suspected for some time that Levi was more than he appeared. Worse, he must've listened to his insatiable ramblings for him—how much he wanted Levi under him begging for more. Jacques hated his disadvantage. That would be corrected should they beat the odds and succeed in escaping.

"We all will escape. That's all I want." Levi said and

then whispered some words as he touched the barred door to the cage. A metallic click rang out as the lock opened. "Don't try to grab me, please. Hear me out."

Ignoring Levi's request, Jacques pulled him into his arms, holding him so tight to prevent him from escaping. "Don't waste your words on me. Forgiveness will never come from me. You are the only real fool here, young high priest."

"What do you mean?" Levi asked trembling.

"What the fuck are you doing, Jacques?" Reno demanded. "He's trying to help us."

"Bullshit. This has to be another ruse to get us to comply with him." Jacques turned his attention back to Levi. "I'll hand it to you. It took a lot of guts and skill to get past the guards and into here without every warning bell in creation going off. Quite impressive, babe."

"Thank you for calling me 'babe', Jacques." Levi slumped into his hold, showing no resistance.

He released him. "You're not lying?"

Levi shook his head. "No. The guards are under a sleep spell I learned. I also dismantled the spells to this place. It wasn't hard."

God, he was like no one Jacques had ever known, as a captive or as a free immortal long ago. There was real courage inside Levi.

Jacques stepped back from the high priest. He wouldn't let him get to him anymore than he already had. Besides, this was likely some trick. Feandan might've put Levi up to this, or at least manipulated him to risk everything. The cruelty of Feandan exceeded all who came before him. The bastard could use Levi to gain their trust to learn any plans they might've cooked up for an escape. Once known,

Feandan would enjoy delivering punishment to him and the shade.

"No, Jacques," Levi said. "Feandan knows nothing of this."

"Stay out of my head, Levi." He turned his back to the man whom he couldn't stop thinking about. Every waking moment since that first time Levi consumed every thought —and even in sleep Jacques dreamed about him.

"You believe you can get us out of here?" Reno asked.

Levi whispered, "Yes. I do."

Jacques whirled back around, taking hold of Levi by his wrists. "The shade may be a sucker, but I'm not. Even if I believed you, which I don't, there's more to the spells holding us than you know. You will be killed the minute we step out of this cell. We will suffer incredible pain at Feandan's hand and you will be executed."

"Let him go or I swear you'll have to deal with me," Reno growled.

Jacques didn't move to release Levi.

"I'm so sorry," Levi said, as tears rolled down his cheeks.

Completely floored, Jacques released his wrists. "You're not lying, are you?"

"No. I'm not."

"Okay then." Jacques felt like the world had suddenly stopped spinning. Up was down and down was up. "I believe you."

"Now that we have that settled," Reno said. "What's your plan, sweetheart?"

"I don't know how much time we have so we better hurry." Levi glanced at the wooden door and then back at him and Reno. "I read about a portal spell in the Book of Timu. I haven't been able to perform it, but it says most immortals can create portals. Is that true?"

"Sorry, sweetheart. I'm new to my immortal life. I don't know much magic at all," Reno said. "And my buddy here hasn't been really instructive these past few weeks."

Levi turned from Reno to him. "So? Is it true? Can you make a portal we can escape through?"

Jacques didn't answer but thought, *Does he really mean to try this insanity? Why? What's his angle?*

"No angle," Levi answered. "I swear."

Jacques cupped Levi's chin. "Even though I believe you now, Levi, you've got to stay out of my head."

Levi stepped back from him, trembling. "I'm sorry, but I don't know how I'm doing it. Believe me, if I did I would've stopped it a long time ago."

"Quiet your mind," he ordered. "Think about some time or place that you enjoy. Don't let your thoughts wander."

Levi closed his eyes. "Is it something like meditation?"

"Yes. Control your thoughts." Easy to ask of someone so young, but hard to expect. It'd taken him a century or more to learn how to do just that. But in the past few weeks, just being near Levi had undone much of that control.

"I think it's working. I can't hear either of your thoughts." He opened his eyes. "Thank you."

"You're wasting time, which I doubt we have much of."

Reno smiled. "*We?* That sounds like you're in, Jacques."

"I am in."

"Good," the shade said. "Then it's time to saddle up and get the hell out of here."

"Yes it is," Jacques agreed. "Levi is right. Creating a portal is a simple spell, but I don't have enough power left to open one large enough for a mosquito to pass through."

"I thought of that ." Levi stepped right between him and Reno.

"And?" Reno asked.

"We need to open a portal," Levi answered, taking his and Reno's hands. "Maybe with your help I can do it."

Even though Jacques believed Levi, he wasn't about to let him call the shots any longer. In a flash, he grabbed Levi's arm and pulled him in close, covering his mouth with his hand. "Got you."

"What the fuck, Jacques?" Reno's tone held a dangerous warning. "Let him go, right now."

"He may be having a change of heart for the time being, Reno, but if we're going to really get free of this place you're going to have to trust me, okay?"

"Why should I trust you, phantom?" Reno was clearly about to pounce. "Why should I trust anyone?"

"You shouldn't." Jacques turned his attention back to Levi. "I'm going to remove my hand from your mouth. Don't scream."

Levi nodded.

God, he loved holding Levi immobile next to him. His scent filled his nostrils, notes of lemon and raindrops.

"If you make one wrong move, I will snap your neck." Jacques lied.

He could never kill Levi, even if everything logical inside told him he should. Something about Levi made him the sexy high priest's hostage, not the other way around. Jacques knew it, but Levi would never know.

CHAPTER 7

33) LISTEN to the words of the angel, Rajiah: Behold the unbreakable union of bloodliner, angel, and jinn. Though quite rare, some triads reach perfection. 34) From their holy union, the bloodliner receives immortality, and the angel and jinn receive power immeasurable. 35) Can The Dark and the Rogues form such a union? I asked. 36) Tis true, Timu. Such immortals can join with a bloodliner for such a union, but it is not easily done for any immortals, whether angel and jinn, demon and ifrit, or phantom and shade. 37) Many have sought to create such a triad, but few have succeeded. The mystery is beyond even immortals to understand.

The Book of Timu: Verses 33 through 37—Chapter 13

───

Levi had made a foolish mistake, now he would pay with his life.

"Did you not hear me the first time, Jacques?" Reno's scowl showed he meant business. "Let him go, or else you will have to deal with me."

He couldn't see Jacques's face since the phantom held him with his back to his front, but he prayed the immortal would concede to Reno and release him. But Jacques's hand remained over his mouth.

His and Reno's thoughts were no longer accessible to him. Jacques had urged him to quiet his mind and stay out of his head. It had worked moments ago. Now, his mind was anything but *quiet,* even though the power to hear their thoughts no longer worked.

"And you'll do exactly what to me?" Jacques shot back to Reno. "I've got centuries of experience on my side. What do you have, newborn-shade?"

"I may not know much, but I have enough to take you out. I sense that the energy left inside you is much less than what I have left." Reno's eyes narrowed. "Experience or not, that has to tip the scales to my side."

With Reno's help, Levi might wiggle out of this mess.

Jacques tightened his hold on him. "If we don't fuck him right now, all of his effort, whether sincere or not, will be for nothing."

Four of Jacques's words reverberated in Levi's head. *Fuck. Him. Right. Now.* His anxiety mushroomed, but his cock betrayed him and swelled.

Reno edged forward. "You're lying."

"If you don't believe me, listen to him. Levi, are you calm now?"

He wasn't but nodded, hoping they would believe the lie.

Jacques removed his hand from his mouth, but kept his body restrained with his muscular arms. Clearly, he had no plans to release him. No way could he break free of such strength. Pushing his luck with him would be suicide, and he didn't have a death wish.

"Tell him," Jacques commanded. "If we don't get power from a completed tripling, this idiotic plan of yours will fail."

Levi hadn't thought of that possibility. The past several days, he'd been consumed with getting Reno and Jacques free from the Conclave. He'd worked out so many details, including his own exit from the Conclave once the immortals were free, turning over the book to Eric Langley, a bloodliner on the outside, the spell for the guards, making sure Feandan was away, and more. How could he have missed that neither Reno nor Jacques would have enough power to open a magical portal—*without tripling with him?*

Clearly, Jacques would need power to create a portal for them to escape through, and that meant sex. And this time, he would have to come inside him. They both would. Dizziness and his pent-up fantasies and desires to be overwhelmed by the two immortals kept coherent thought at bay for several seconds.

Once his mind finally cleared, he tilted his head toward Reno. "He's telling the truth."

Jacques squeezed him tight. "Good job, babe."

Reno didn't look convinced but did stop edging forward. "So, we're going to make love to him here and now."

"Wait a second." Levi's words came out shaky and fast. "This isn't what I planned. There's got to be another way.

"You still think you're in charge, high priest? That ended the moment you walked into this cell." Jacques's sarcasm stung him to the core. "Yes we're going to fuck. Here and now."

In a microsecond, Jacques had ripped off his clothes. The air touched his skin, and gooseflesh appeared everywhere. The hunger grew to a roar inside Levi. He wanted them to overwhelm him. In fact, he'd dreamed about it since the first night with them.

Jacques massaged his nipples with his free hand, circling the tiny bits of flesh but never actually touching the tips. Tingles danced on his skin as the tiny buds hardened.

"Buddy, I get it." Reno tilted his head. "Sex gives us immortals power, but can you slow down some?"

"No. We need to power up and fast. Lengthy foreplay isn't part of the equation." Jacques turned his head to face him. "You are not to come until I say so, Levi."

"I don't understand. According to the book, the triangle needs all three...umm...*participants* to climax for the power to be created for the two immortals." He wasn't about to say *lovers,* even though that was how he remembered the text.

Jacques slapped his ass. It stung, but his control and dominance made him even harder.

"What the hell!" Reno's hands curled into fists.

"You want out of here, you better let me do this my way." Jacques pinched Levi's nipple. "Don't question me again, understand?"

"I won't," he whimpered. "I swear."

Jacques's dominant nature unraveled and fascinated him, and he wasn't about to push back. Too dangerous. Besides, he really liked it.

Jacques massaged his ass with his right hand, while his left continued to hold him captive. Levi's hunger sped past his worry about their predicament.

Jacques's hand came up from behind him, between his legs, and then his fingers wrapped around his balls, sending a jolt of heat through his body. No longer a prisoner, Jacques was in full command of the moment as well as his body.

Levi couldn't help but moan.

"Cowboy, he's ready," Jacques said in a lusty tone that drove Levi crazy with desire.

"Yes he is." Reno grinned. "Nice and hard."

Levi shook from head to toe as Reno began stroking his cock and Jacques squeezed his balls from behind.

"We both have to be inside you to make the connection really work," Jacques said.

Levi nodded. "Okay."

"We need lube."

"It's on that table outside the cell," he told Jacques.

"Don't move a muscle."

Again, he nodded.

All his senses jumped with pleasure and panic as Jacques let go of him and walked out of the cell. When he returned and began applying lubrication to his ass, Levi felt like he might actually lose his mind.

The cock, Jacques's cock, Levi had tasted, teased, and felt inside his mouth during the past few weeks was fully erect, a massive thing, and pressing between his ass cheeks.

"Ready?" Jacques asked with an unexpected gentle tone.

Did he actually have another side to him, a softer side? Levi believed he might. But how could anyone get past his layers of pain to uncover it? Not him, a high priest of the very people that had piled torture after torture on top of Jacques over the centuries. Buzzing with want, he decided one night with the dark immortal was a small price to pay for his people's crimes as well as his own.

"I'm ready."

Without hesitation, Jacques lifted his body like it was a feather.

Levi's feet dangled more than two feet from the floor. Slowly he lowered him down to the ground until Levi was crouching on his hands and knees, facing Reno, who had pulled down his jeans to his ankles exposing his thick, hard dick.

Reno's chocolate brown eyes locked with his. "Put your arms around my waist, sweetheart."

Levi obeyed, loving the feel of his muscled frame.

"Good," Jacques said. "Now, lean back into me."

Jacques's dominance over him sent electrical sparks racing up and down his spine. How could the sexy phantom be so strong after being held captive for so long? Levi wondered exactly what was the depth of the strength that lived inside him. He could feel Jacques's breath skate over his back, causing his desire to multiply exponentially.

Jacques's tone sharpened. "Did you not hear me, high priest?"

"Yes. I heard you. Lean back. I know." Unsteady with desire, Levi did his best to comply.

"That's it, babe." Jacques fingered his ass pushing past the tight ring.

As the initial sting shot through him, Levi remembered to breath, as they'd helped him learn at their previous encounters. The pain subsided quickly and his lust for them ramped up.

"Lick the shade's cock," Jacques ordered.

"Okay," Levi whispered and began running his tongue up and down Reno's shaft.

"That feels so good, sweetheart," Reno groaned.

As Jacques spread his ass cheeks and began pressing into him with that massive cock of his, Levi could feel his pulse in his own dick.

Jacques's mouth went to his ear. "Remember, you are not to come unless I say."

"How could I hold back? Shouldn't we hurry this up before—"

Jacques tugged his hair, making it clear who was really in charge. "Listen carefully. I will not repeat myself. We need a lot of power to open a portal. Hold back until I say so. Got it, babe?"

Somehow, he had to obey Jacques. "Yes. I got it."

But even now, Levi thought his advancing climax could crash through his will. *I must wait.* His immortal phantom deserved that. And more. As he swallowed Reno to the back of his throat, he tried to focus his thoughts in the hopes of not coming.

Jacques saw him as the enemy, and Levi knew he would never see him or Reno again once Jacques had enough power to create the portal for the two of them to escape through. That thought broke his heart but also kept his desires from overwhelming him. Still, feeling Jacques's dick pressing against his ass and Reno's cock slipping over his tongue renewed the heat building inside him. He couldn't hold back much longer even if he wanted to obey his phantom.

Jacques leaned over him, biting his earlobe. "Take in as deep breath as you can."

Levi inhaled every bit of air he could.

"Good, babe," Jacques said. "Now let it out nice and slow."

Again, Levi did as he was told.

When the last bit of oxygen left his lips, Jacques shifted his pelvis forward, slowly driving that massive dick deep into his body. The pressure grew and grew as each inch of his phantom's cock pierced him.

Jacques kissed the back of his neck. "Breathe, babe."

Again, he couldn't resist his commands. As he refilled

his lungs, Jacques took full possession of his ass with long, slow strokes. In and out. He could feel his leg muscles tighten as his phantom drove deeper still into him, turning the tables and making him the sacrifice. Without hesitation, Levi took it. How he'd dreamed of this, and now a burn grew inside him for more. Embers stirred. Electrical explosions streaked through him.

As Jacques continued, in and out, over and over, he roared, "You will never deny me what I want, high priest. Never again."

"Keep it down," Reno said. "We don't need to wake the entire Conclave."

Jacques stiffened at Reno's words. The pumping action inside Levi stopped. Then Jacques pulled out of his body.

Instinctively, Levi tried to shift back into him to keep his cock inside his body.

"No. You are not in charge anymore." His eyes narrowed. "For that attempt, you will be punished. Later."

Not in charge? Punished? Later? Jacques's words both scared and thrilled him at the same time. Did Jacques mean to take him through the portal with him and Reno? But what would it be like being their prisoner?

Suddenly, he picked up Reno's thoughts.

Jacques, do you see that red light around him?

Yes. The sexy phantom shot back.

What is it?

I don't know.

Their thoughts were back, and that pleased Levi very much. Could they hear his thoughts? *I hope not.*

With his enormous hands, Jacques guided Levi into a standing position. "To make the best connection for power with Levi, you're going to have to take his cock while I fuck him."

With brown eyes wide and inviting. Reno smiled and cupped Levi's chin. "Sounds perfect to me. Toss me that lube."

Jacques pitched the bottle to Reno, who popped the top and squirted a healthy amount into his palm.

"Sweetheart, I want every part of you," Reno said with a kiss, and then began slicking up his cock.

When his immortal mouth came down on his left nipple, Levi felt tingles sizzle inside him. The thrill weakened his knees, and if Jacques hadn't been holding him from behind he might've fallen. When Reno moved to the other nipple as he continued stroking his dick, Levi could feel his climax coming.

"Lie back, shade," Jacques instructed, once again demonstrating his dominance.

Reno stretched out on the ground in front of Levi, lifting his legs high and revealing his gorgeous ass.

Then Levi felt Jacques squeeze his balls tightly from behind. "No coming until I say."

He nodded, determined to obey him. But the force inside him felt like a soon-to-erupt volcano that wouldn't be denied its release of heat and energy.

Jacques guided him down to Reno, who crushed his lips with his mouth. The kiss went on and on, as Jacques thrust back into his body.

Reno used his hand to guide Levi's dick into his hungry ass. "Fuck me, sweetheart. I want every inch of you."

Insane with lust, Levi thrust into Reno, feeling the grip of his sexy shade's body on his dick.

"That's it," Reno breathed. "Feels amazing."

Jacques got in sync with his rhythm stroke for stroke, thrusting into Levi.

"God, this feels so good," Levi admitted aloud. His head

spun, and hot flares streaked back and forth from their bodies—from Jacques through him to Reno and back again. The heat rose exponentially, burning him through and through. He'd never dreamt that being with them would be this incredible. So consuming.

A crash in the other room shocked him. *Feanda!? Guards! Oh no!*

"We have to come now!" Jacques roared, thrusting deep inside his body and pushing him deeper into Reno.

The jolt sent shockwaves rolling through Levi, and the pleasure that followed besieged every cell inside his body. The door burst open, but he didn't look to see who came. He knew. No way did he or his two immortals have a chance to survive. *Please, don't let this end this way.*

"Now!" Jacques commanded, shooting his cream inside him.

Reno yelled. "Coming!"

Everything inside Levi blazed red-hot. His body tightened from head to toe, as he exploded like a volcano into Reno. Suddenly, the colors of the rainbow swirled around the three of them.

"Chain the immortals and kill Levi!" Feandan screamed.

CHAPTER 8

RENO WATCHED in amazement as Jacques's outstretched hand shot several spheres of silver light at the guards and Feandan. They all recoiled backward, trying to avoid the phantom's magic missiles. Some succeeded like Feandan. Some did not and their bodies vanished.

Unlocking from their final sexual encounter, he and Jacques guided Levi behind them, blocking him from the approaching assholes. No one would ever harm Levi, not on his watch.

Reno could sense Levi's body vibrating behind him and Jacques's body heating beside him. His own body felt strange to him—strong and powerful like never before. Something astonishing had occurred when the three of them had come together. What? He didn't know. He looked at Jacques.

What happened? He sent to the phantom.

Jacques shrugged. *A power exchange, but on a scale I didn't know was possible. Doesn't matter right now. You've got to keep Feandan and his buddies at bay with your own power until I can open a portal.*

How do I do that?

Concentrate. Can't you feel the power inside you from our tripling with the high priest?

I feel something. Warmth.

Look with your mind at the center of your body. You'll see it.

Reno concentrated and saw a spinning sphere of gray smoke. *Hell, I must be Smokey the Immortal. Yes, I see it.*

You're a shade. That's how your magic looks. Use it.

Feandan's voice sounded raspy and full of rage. "Kill the traitor Levi! The monsters are feeding off his power. Once he's dead, we can subdue the immortals."

Reno glanced at Levi, who seemed quite courageous at the odds they were facing. Fuck the odds. No one was harming Levi as long as Reno had breath in his body.

Using only his will, Reno tried to guide his magic to his hands. Now what? He didn't have time to figure out what to do next. Damn it. He was a soldier not a wizard. What he really needed was a gun. He understood guns.

Suddenly, the smoky magic shot from his fingers, each pulse forming into a bullet-shaped missile that flew at the advancing bloodliners. The explosion that followed blinded him, but their screams told him that it had worked.

Jacques sent, *Let's go.*

Reno looked at what had been the back wall of the cell and found an opening—a magical portal to some place other than here. Together, he and Jacques carried Levi to their escape.

"Nooo!" Feandan shouted.

Then silence.

For a split-second, Reno felt as if they were spinning on a massive rollercoaster.

The next instant, the feeling passed as he felt solid ground under his feet.

He grinned. "That was different."

Levi pushed against Jacques's chest with his hands. "You did it."

Jacques stepped back, releasing their intertwined embrace. "If, high priest, you mean by *did it* that I created a portal to escape through, then yes, I did it."

Reno felt him stiffen. The phantom's harsh tone had impacted Levi.

"Jacques, cool it," Reno stated flatly. "Where are we?"

Scanning the area, he guessed it to be some kind of cave or mine. The air smelled dank but seemed harmless. A few slivers of light from various holes in the rocky ceiling dimly illuminated the area. Reno wondered if it was magic light or sunshine from outside.

"My place."

"I'm surprised it still exists after all your years of imprisonment."

"Me, too."

Levi opened his mouth, and then shut it tight. What was he going to say?

Reno wished he knew, but instead of asking he turned back to Jacques. "Why here?"

"You ask too many questions, shade. Ask him." The grumpy immortal pointed to Levi. "He's read the book."

Levi sighed, clearly just as unsure of what was going to happen next as he was. "Portals are tricky, Reno." Levi covered his naked crotch with his hands, his modesty returning quickly despite all they'd shared together. "Best to create one to a place the spell caster knows well."

"I've got a lot to learn about this magic crap." Reno

turned to the phantom, who was looking around the space. "You got a place for us to sit? Maybe some clothes?"

"I did, but they're all dust by now." Jacques closed his eyes.

Reno heard some crackling and felt something akin to electricity in the air. Suddenly, a couple of leather chairs appeared in the middle of the cavern.

Now wearing a black shirt, blue jeans, and hiking boots, Jacques gestured to the new furniture. "Be my guest."

"Pretty cool trick," Reno said, hoping to lighten the mood. "Impressive."

"If you want to clothe the high priest, do it yourself. You have your own power." Jacques continued his inspection of the cave. "But if I were you, I'd leave him just the way he is. Your choice, for now."

Reno thought about it. He did like his eyes to have full-access to Levi's incredible body, but he needed time and rest.

Jacques turned to Levi. "Don't even think about trying to leave. Understand?"

Levi's eyes widened. "Where would I go?"

Without a word, the phantom started to walk down the tunnel.

Reno's irritation grew with each footfall of the self-appointed general. "Where are you going?"

Jacques stopped and turned back around. "To get provisions. Mine are all long gone, I'm certain."

"Why not use magic like you did with the chairs?" he asked.

"I could, but it doesn't really quench thirst or ease hunger. It's only illusion. Enough questions. Figure the rest out for yourself." Jacques turned around and marched away.

Reno called out, "I'd like a porterhouse with a baked potato."

Levi grinned at his mockery of Jacques.

That pleased Reno.

"How long will you be gone?" Levi yelled after the phantom.

"As long as it takes, high priest," Jacques yelled back.

Reno pulled Levi in close and squeezed him, loving the feel of his skin against his. "If you're not back in an hour, we'll come looking for you."

"You're learning," Jacques shouted back as he turned a corner disappearing from sight.

The years in the Conclave's cell had likely changed Jacques. He decided the guy deserved some space. God knew even his short time in the cell had changed him. Reno silently vowed to never take his freedom for granted.

Levi broke from his hold and took a couple steps away. "Can you conjure clothes for us?"

Reno took a hard, long look at Levi. "Not sure. It might take me some time to get it right."

With Jacques gone, he would have Levi all to himself.

CHAPTER 9

LEVI WOKE, but kept his eyes shut. The reality of what had happened and where he had ended up whirled like a top in his mind.

As long as Levi could remember, his life had been planned for him. How could he have ever expected that meeting Jacques and Reno would destroy those plans? He thought about the life he'd left. He'd always felt alien in the Conclave, out of place. But now? Levi's new found freedom frightened him.

He recalled a passage that he'd ran across a few nights after his first time with Jacques and Reno, a passage he couldn't ever forget.

It mentioned something called a "Perfect Triad" that allowed the bloodliner to cheat death entirely, becoming immortal—just like the shades and phantoms and other immortal beings. *Have I been changed from bloodliner to monster? Was that what had happened to me during the tripling with Jacques and Reno?*

The silk sheet that Reno had created earlier was wrapped around Levi's body. The bed the shade had also made felt amazingly soft. No clothes though for either of them. Reno had tried, but failed.

Levi had made an effort to stay awake, but his exhaustion had easily pushed him into sleep. *How long have I been asleep?*

"Levi, you okay?" Reno asked.

He opened his eyes and turned to where the shade's voice was coming.

Reno sat in one of the leather chairs, his stare fixed on him. God, he looked so strong and powerful. Not a monster but instead a naked Greek god.

He wanted Reno again, no denying it. From the first time Levi had met the shade, he'd sensed an immeasurable goodness within him. Could his instinct about him be wrong?

"I'm fine." Levi sat up, and the sheet fell away, exposing his naked frame. "The rest helped."

Reno stood, and Levi saw his cock lengthen.

Looking at the sexy man's body, Levi felt heat rushing into his cheeks. He pulled the sheet back up to cover his own body. "Is Jacques back?" he asked, hoping to calm down.

"No. But I am here," Reno said with a tone of hunger.

A shiver shot up and down Levi's spine. His desire blasted through him like a blowtorch and his cock stiffened.

Reno waved his hand, and Levi's silk covering flew off of him to the end of the bed. "I'm really getting the hang of this magic thing, don't you think?"

Levi looked him straight in the eyes. "Why did you do it?"

Reno grinned wickedly. "I want to touch and taste every part of you, sweetheart."

The blood flowing through his veins felt like hot lava. "But we need Jacques for you to gain more energy."

Reno shook his head. "Fuck that. We can triple with the grump another time. Besides, I still have energy to spare from what happened back in the cell."

Emotions rolled through Levi. He craved Reno to possess him, to pleasure him. Levi also wanted to pleasure Reno. Still, he wanted to know the shade's reason for coupling. "Why? Why now?"

In a flash, Reno slipped onto the bed, curling up next to him. "I've wanted you from the moment I met you. You don't give yourself enough credit. Look what you did. You've righted a wrong, my love."

He called me 'my love.' That thrilled him. "How could I not at least try to do something to spring you?"

"Levi, you are amazing. Look how long Jacques was held before someone showed him compassion. Without your courage, I could've been a prisoner as long as he was."

Levi's guilt returned. "The escape attempt could've ended badly."

"But it didn't. I bet you're the first to ever try. Others must've felt the injustice of it before, but did nothing."

Reno probably was right.

Levi had never heard of any other high priest making such an attempt.

"You're one of a kind, honey." Reno's fingers traced his chin, and then he kissed his shoulder. "Your skin is delicious."

Reno guided him onto his side, positioning his front against Levi's back.

When Levi felt Reno's cock pressing against his ass, sparks shot through his entire body. Reno worked on the tightness in his neck with one hand, and with the other he cupped Levi's balls, squeezing gently.

Unable to control himself, Levi moaned.

"You like me touching you this way, sweetheart?" Reno asked.

"Y-Yes. Feels good."

"How about here?" Reaching around him, Reno tweaked his nipples.

Nothing in his life had ever felt so right as Reno's touch.

"Perfect, Reno," he said, stroking his cock with one hand and reaching behind to do the same to Reno's dick.

Reno rolled him onto his back. His chocolate eyes didn't blink, and his mouth curled up into the most amazing smile Levi had ever seen. His immortal lover leaned down and planted a long, lingering kiss on him. Levi parted his lips for Reno's advancing tongue to probe him, imagining more of him entering his needy body.

Reno pulled him in closer to his muscled frame while he deepened their kiss. Feeling their hard cocks pressing against each other, Levi's body turned to a warm mass of sweet anticipation of what was to come.

Reno broke his amazing kiss, and Levi instantly missed his lips on him.

"Sweetheart, you're incredible," Reno said.

"So are you," he responded with a breathy moan. "If you and Jacques hadn't...I just...I just don't know what..."

"You saved us, too, honey."

"But after all I did...and the Conclave did..." The guilt came crashing back into him like a sledgehammer. "I don't deserve..."

Reno placed his index finger to his lips. "You took a great risk to help us escape. That's enough. I've never met a man like you. You were a prisoner as much as we were."

Levi couldn't hold back the tears. He could've gotten them all killed.

Reno pulled him in close. "Sweetheart, tell me what to do to make you feel better."

"Make love to me," he told him. "Please."

"Gladly, my love."

Reno leaned down, and gave him a tender kiss.

In that very moment his toes curled, Levi suddenly believed that everything would be okay. But was that really possible? Would Jacques, now free, triple with him and Reno again? Not likely. He hated the suffering Jacques had been dealt by the hands of his predecessors.

"Do you think Jacques will return?" he asked, even though he thought he already knew the answer.

"Considering what he's been through, I'm not surprised by his dark mood," Reno said. "Still, I believe he's okay deep down. He'll be there for us, just you wait and see."

"You're the eternal optimist, literally." Levi touched Reno's naked, solid chest. "I hope you're right."

"I am," Reno said, grinning. "But right now, I want you for myself. Tripling for power with Jacques can come later. Much later." He tweaked his nipples again.

Levi felt the bits of flesh harden under his naughty treatment. Gooseflesh popped on his exposed skin. Reno knew just what to touch, when to touch, how to touch. "But shouldn't we...wait for..."

"Shh. Right now, isn't about tripling. It's only about you and me. I want to explore all of you. Since that first time with you, I've dreamed of this moment. I want to get you so turned on, you'll think you've gone to heaven." Reno swallowed his nipple.

Electricity traveled from where Reno sucked all the way

to Levi's cock and balls. Reno's mouth left one nipple, only to swallow the other.

Levi thrashed on the bed and fisted the sheet.

Back and forth, Reno bathed his chest with his tongue, causing his cock to throb like mad and moans to escape his mouth.

"That's it." Reno's words came hotly. "Let go, my love."

"Oh, yes."

"I can't wait for my dick to be inside you, filling you up." Reno held out his empty hand, and suddenly a bottle of lube appeared.

"P-Please, I want it." Levi's body buzzed with blistering lust.

Reno applied lubricant to his fingers and then began slicking up Levi's tight ass ring. Then Reno moved down and licked at his navel, while continuing to stretch his backside.

Even though Levi couldn't withstand much more, his sexy immortal continued his mouth torment going down until his hot breath skated over his cock and balls.

Reno kissed the tip of his dick, while slipping a finger into his ass. The sensations in Levi's body increased. Where he'd been warm before, now he was ablaze with heat.

Fuck, he's so wonderfully tight! Reno's thoughts were loud and demanding. *I can't wait to be inside him again.*

Levi caught his breath and held it. Reno's thoughts rushed in like a stampede. *How the hell am I hearing his thoughts again? How does it work?*

Reno froze and looked at him. "That's weird."

"What?"

"I can hear your thoughts, too."

"Shit! I mean, shoot."

Reno laughed. "No, I think you did mean 'shit.'"

Unable to hold back, Levi shot him a grin.

Reno stroked his cock. "My love, I want you to feel pleasure like never before."

Levi felt every muscle tighten when Reno swallowed his cock and thrust into him with his thick finger. He widened his legs, as Reno sucked on him like a man dying of thirst.

"Reno, I-I'm so close."

Reno slipped his mouth off of Levi's cock. "Come for me, sweetheart."

His commanding thought and his sexy lips on him shoved Levi over the edge. Unable to stop himself, Levi dug his nails into Reno's flesh. He came hard, erupting down his immortal's mouth.

Reno drank down every drop.

Levi pounded the bed with his fists. "Y-yesss."

Jacques's voice shocked him. "I see you figured out a way to keep yourselves occupied while I was gone."

CHAPTER 10

JACQUES WATCHED the blood rush to Levi's cheeks.

Reno sat up from between Levi's legs, and then rolled his own legs off the bed to the floor. He didn't stand, but remained seated on the bed, next to Levi.

While Levi looked rested and satisfied, the shade looked lusty and sweltering.

Levi pulled the sheet up, and his naked body from the neck down vanished from view.

Jacques hated that he could no longer enjoy Levi's beauty—a male beauty that drove him mad with desire.

"Buddy, did you bring the food?" Reno asked. "I'm starving."

"I did." He sat the bags he carried on the bed. "Water, too."

Reno dove in like a starving animal, ripping the paper sacks to pieces. The donuts and bottled water exploded onto the bed. The shade swallowed one cinnamon roll in two bites before moving to another pastry.

Levi didn't move or look at Reno. Instead, his blue eyes

fixed on him. He had to be starving, too. Was he waiting for permission?

Jacques cock hardened, knowing that was exactly what Levi was waiting for. He craved more of his submission. The years of pain and anguish from being subdued against his will seemed to melt into nothingness next to Levi's demonstration of obedience. Everything about the gorgeous man undid him.

"Eat, high priest."

Levi shot him a quick smile that sent him to the moon. Joining the shade in the feast, Levi sat up. The sheet fell away, exposing his naked frame. He could see a drop of his cream ooze out of his cock's slit, which caused Jacques's dick to stiffen. He was consumed with desire to taste that salty bead.

Levi grabbed a chocolate covered donut and began devouring it. Poor thing must've been famished. But why should he even care?

He should hate Levi, who was part of the Conclave-- and not just part of it, but its high priest. Still, how could he fault him? And Levi had put himself at risk to rescue them. Foolish, but Jacques couldn't help but admire his courage. If they'd been a second later on completing the tripling, he and the shade would be back in chains and Levi would be dead as Feandan had ordered.

Jacques clenched his jaw. He had plans for the bastard that included a long, tedious, horrible death. He'd already begun working it out. With the energy he now had, how could Feandan escape his wrath?

The power surging through him felt incredible. A massive sphere of silver light spun in his core. Levi had given that to him and the same amount to Reno, though the shade's power came as a ball of gray smoke.

Centuries had passed since Jacques's last full tripling. Still, he recalled that none of the previous triads had provided so much energy. Not even close. And what about Levi's bloodliner light changing from red into every color of the rainbow shooting in every direction? What did that mean?

"Thanks, buddy," Reno said to him, leaving the bed and taking one of the chairs. "This is good." The shade downed half a bottle of water.

"Don't you have anything to say to me?" Jacques barked at Levi.

He looked up at him, a single chocolate spot on the corner of his lips. "Yes. Thank you."

Jacques's lust went into overdrive. He didn't need to triple for power, though more would be welcomed, but he craved to have Levi with Reno again. But he needed answers first.

"High priest, our tripling in the cell was *unique*. Why?" he demanded.

Levi shrugged and looked away.

Jacques sensed he was holding something back. He grabbed his chin and forced Levi to look at him. "Don't make me ask again."

"Okay. Okay. I could be wrong, but I think we created a Perfect Triad. It's in the Book of Timu."

Jacques struggled with the possibility. *No!* He'd thought such things were only myth. The ramifications boiled into his bones.

"A Perfect what?" Reno asked. "And what's this Book of *Timo*?"

"Book of Timu," Levi corrected. "It's the book about all immortals. A Perfect Triad is where a human bloodliner and two immortals are sealed together, forever."

"So there's something in this book that describes what happened to the three of us?" Reno asked.

"Maybe." Levi closed his eyes and began to recite the passage. "'Behold the unbreakable union of bloodliner, angel, and jinn. A Perfect Triad. From their holy union—'"

"I know the passages, high priest," Jacques interrupted. "But it also says that many have sought to create such a triad, but few have succeeded. The mystery is beyond even immortals to understand."

"I know that, but what other explanation is there?"

The shade rubbed his head. "I don't understand any of this. Angels are real, too?"

"Yes they are, and demons and ifrit and jinn, too. Why would you understand anything, newborn?" Jacques shot back and pointed at Levi. "It means we cannot triple with any human but him. Ever."

"That's okay with me." Reno sat back in the chair, stretching his arms wide. "What else is in the book about this Perfect Triad thing, Levi?"

"Well, according to the Book of Timu, I might not ever die."

"That seems like a good thing to me." Reno looked back at him. "Isn't it?"

Jacques didn't respond. Part of him wanted Levi to be correct. It would mean never having to let him go. Another part, the darker part hated that he would be bonded to Levi for all time.

Reno sighed relief. "Yep. If it really happened, it's a good thing. I know it. Levi knows it. You know it, Jacques. We all know it." The shade returned to the bed, putting his arm protectively around Levi. "I felt a strong bond during our tripling before the escape. Thought I was losing it. Glad I'm not. So Jacques, what's the downside?"

"Plenty, but that can be a discussion for later." He glared at Levi, hoping to make his point quite clear. "Time to pay for your meal, high priest. Stand up."

"What do you mean?" Levi asked in a timid voice. "And why are you frowning?"

The old memories poured into Jacques like a hurricane —the unending suffering, the lack of control, and the humiliation. They all felt terribly fresh.

"High priest, you didn't stand as I commanded you. You'll be punished for your disobedience. Get up on your feet, now!"

Levi leapt from the bed in a single bound. Everything inside Jacques urged him forward to touch Levi, take him, and fill him. He willed his desires into a tenuous surrender.

"Hold on, buddy." Reno jumped in front of Levi and held up his hands to him. "What's this all about?"

"I'm going to set the pecking order straight with him right now," Jacques stated, feeling his cock stiffen in the pants he'd conjured earlier. "Levi has been trained for his whole life to be in charge of our kind, to increase our desire, only to withhold release and pleasure. That's over. You can join me or not. I don't care."

Reno stood his ground, clearly ready to battle him. "You'll not hurt him. Not while I'm here."

"It's okay," Levi said, stepping around Reno and getting in between them. "He's right. It's necessary."

The look on Reno's face showed he was confused. "You're up for this?"

Levi nodded.

"He's more than up for it." Jacques hungered for another tripling with Levi and Reno. Damn, just seeing their naked bodies loaded Jacques's balls up to the max. "Look, shade. He's hard right now just thinking about it."

Reno glanced down at Levi's cock and his eyes filled with lust. "This is what you really want?"

Sheepishly, he nodded.

Jacques watched as the shade's cock lengthened.

Reno pulled Levi into his arms and began fisting his stiff, beautiful dick. Levi immediately did the same to him. The two of them looked incredible to Jacques. He could enjoy watching them jack each other off all night, but that wasn't what he really needed to happen.

"I'm game then," Reno said, releasing his hold on the high priest. "Whatever he wants."

If Jacques was to be tethered to another immortal for a permanent triad, he didn't mind it being Reno. The guy had heart, strength, and smarts. In the cell, he'd actually come to believe the shade might survive with him for a couple of centuries. Plus, Jacques liked him, but he didn't want him to know that. Not yet.

"Good. If the high priest is right and we three are sealed together, he needs to understand how things will operate from now on. We'll start by helping him learn that he cannot come until you or I say so."

"Okay, I guess," Reno said, clearly confused. "Weird, but okay."

Levi didn't move a muscle.

Jacques liked his obedience, thrived on it, in fact. "What did you think of last night, high priest?"

"It was nice," he whispered.

"Nice?"

"I mean great," he answered. "It was great."

"What about the times before?"

He looked down and clasped his hands together. "Not so great. I wish that you could've come with me."

Jacques watched a tear roll down his cheek, which

moved him in ways he didn't think possible. "You should be punished for not letting us come, don't you think?"

Levi nodded. "Yes."

"Add *Sir* to your responses to me from now on. Understand?"

"Yes, Sir."

"Good. Shade, how do you want Levi to address you?"

"I really don't care. *Reno* works just fine."

"No it doesn't. You need something that immediately lets him know you are in charge." Jacques could tell Reno still wasn't convinced. "You fucking have to. He's been programmed by the Conclave. Sure, he seems compliant now. But what if some of their brainwashing kicks in and he betrays us?"

Reno shrugged. "You seem to be running this show, for now. Fine. *Sir* works for me, too."

"I think we both need different handles for him. It will lessen the confusion when he's addressing either of us and we're commanding him."

Reno grinned, fisting his hard cock. "You've got lots of rules, phantom. Okay. How about 'Commander'?"

"Good. And we will call his 'prisoner.'"

Levi let out a little moan. Their talk was clearly turning him on.

Hell, it's getting to me, too. "Prisoner, get on your knees."

Levi dropped to his knees. "Like this, Sir?"

"It's sufficient for now," he answered and then turned to Reno. "So what do you think so far?"

"I can't lie. I kind of like this." Reno touched Levi's cheek. "I'm itching for more from you, sweet...uh...prisoner." Laughter and lust danced in his dark brown eyes. "Jacques, let's get on with it. I can't wait any longer."

"Yes. I can see that."

"I don't think you do, buddy. Whatever this Perfect Triad thing is, I don't know. But together in the cell, you and I and Levi had something incredible. I felt something inside me, so awesome and overwhelming. He gets to me on a level I've never known before. All I want to do is pleasure him and give him all I can."

Levi looked up at the cowboy in a way that screamed utter devotion. "Commander, please. Just do what Sir says. I deserve it...and I need it."

Jacques felt everything inside him tighten with uncontrollable want for Levi, their prisoner.

CHAPTER 11

22) THE SPELL OF PAIN is not easy to master. If done properly, the immortal will be paralyzed by agony until you and your followers can either capture the abomination for the Conclave's ceremonies or kill the abomination to rid the world of another monster.

The History of The Conclave and Journals of High Priests

Still on his knees, Levi shook with excitement and apprehension. What his sexy immortals might have planned put him on edge.

Jacques walked over and cupped his chin, sending an electric flash through his body. When Jacques picked him up and placed him on the bed, Levi could feel his pulse throbbing in his cock.

When Jacques shed his clothes, Levi's gut clenched.

Seeing all the scars over his muscled frame filled Levi

with renewed remorse. He'd seen them before crisscrossing his body, but not like this, fully on display to prove his guilt.

"Look at me, prisoner," Jacques ordered.

"Yes Sir." Levi tried to look directly into his eyes, but his shame wouldn't allow it.

Jacques cupped his chin. "Look at me."

Trembling, he locked eyes with his captor. "Yes, Sir."

Somehow, all of this felt right. Jacques calling him prisoner seemed appropriate. Obeying his commands was right, deserved, and yes, even desired. Turn about was fair play as he'd heard from his Aunt Grace time and again. For her it had meant something completely different. Now, for Levi, it meant those who had once been his prisoners were now his masters. Jacques needed to take him in this manner—with dominance and force. Surrendering fully to him and to Reno was his only hope to not lose his immortals.

"Time for your punishment, prisoner." Jacques lifted him off his feet and placed him on the bed face down. "Now, look at me, prisoner—really look at me."

He turned his head Jacques's direction, keeping the front of his body plastered to the bed. When he saw that Jacques's cock was fully erect, he ground his hips to create friction on his own dick.

Reno moved out of view, to the opposite side of the bed.

Levi imagined how he looked to them, sprawled out between them on the sheets. The thought had him grinding his dick even more into the mattress.

Slap! The sting of Jacques's hand on his ass froze his wiggling to a stop.

"You will not come until I or Commander say. You will not move until I or Commander say. You will not speak, until I or Commander say. Understand, prisoner?"

Levi nodded.

Jacques lifted his hand and what appeared in it sent both a chill and heat through Levi's flesh.

A large paddle.

Levi gulped, knowing that Jacques's plan was to burn his bottom with it for his punishment.

Jacques stared down at him with a face full of determination and strength. And something else. What?

"I think you've earned five strikes for your actions the first night we met and for withholding my pleasure. Five more for the same for Commander. And five more just because I say so. How many is that, prisoner?"

"Fifteen, Sir."

"Good. That's right. You have more coming for the other nights in the cell, but those can wait for another time."

Jacques's strength and willpower blasted Levi into tiny bits of compliance. And sensing the incredible pain that he harbored, how could anyone refuse him?

Reno spoke gently, "Sweetheart...I mean prisoner, are you sure about this?"

His words made Levi pause. Was he sure? Once begun, he knew there was no going back. Ever. Levi dug deep into his mind. Yes, he wanted this, needed this. And Jacques needed it, too. In a different way, so did Reno. He fisted the sheets, knowing that he longed for being with them this way more than anything ever before.

"Answer Commander!" Jacques demanded.

"Yes, Sir. Yes, Commander, I'm ready." His lust burned like liquid steel inside him.

"Don't hesitate. That earned you two more strikes of this paddle." The dominance in Jacques's tone held him to the bed more than any chains could. "What's the count, prisoner?"

"Seventeen, Sir."

"Correct. Shade, hold the paddle. I want him chained."

The extreme urge to press hard into the mattress as Jacques magically created his restraints almost overwhelmed him, but he resisted. That pleased him, knowing he'd obeyed Jacques's command.

He felt the restraints snap onto his wrists and ankles.

Jacques ran his big hand gently over his backside. "I want you to count the strikes as they are delivered on this hot little ass of yours. Understand?"

"Yes, Sir."

Jacques's thought shot out. *Give it a try, Reno.*

Okay. Here it goes.

The little sting of the paddle to his backside smarted slightly. *Too soft.*

"One, Sir. Commander." *I can take more.*

"That's right, prisoner," Jacques said. "Too soft, Reno. Try again."

They can hear my thoughts again?

"Yes we can," Jacques said.

Likely something about us all being meant for each other, Reno sent out.

"Probably, but we can worry about that later," Jacques said aloud. "Shade, can you deliver a harder blow? You heard his thoughts. He wants more. Needs more."

Reno brought the paddle against his ass. *Smack!* This time he felt it. The pain quieted his mind and sent his desire to the stratosphere.

"Two, Sir. Commander."

Three strikes followed in succession.

"Three, four, five, Sir. Commander." Levi felt the heat on his ass cheeks and his lusty tears on his face. Biting his lip, he braced for the next twelve to come. *His punishment.*

They didn't come. Instead, hands massaged everything

away. His cock was so hard he thought he might die. God, he wanted to come. If he didn't soon, he felt as if he might explode into a million pieces. Was this how all the Conclave immortal captives felt? Not just for a single night, for their entire imprisonment. And Jacques had been imprisoned for several lifetimes.

Smack! The last strike was harder and with more sting.

"Six, Sir. Commander."

"Good, prisoner," Reno said, stroking his hair. "Very good."

His kind words and gentle touch thrilled Levi. If he could please him and Jacques, trust them to keep him safe, ease Jacques's pain, soften Reno's memories, everything would snap into place for their new little corner of the world.

Reno asked, "Are you doing okay?"

"Yes, Commander. Very good."

"You want to spank him, Jacques?"

"Let's see what he wants. Tell us, prisoner. You want me to deliver some strikes on that hot ass of yours, make it nice and pink for my dick?"

Gooseflesh popped up on his arms and legs. "Yes, Sir."

"So brave. I'm impressed." Jacques's words melted his hesitation and made him crazed with desire.

"He is amazing. I've never known any man like him." Reno continued stroking his hair.

You're both amazing and wonderful and so much more than I deserve.

"Is that right, prisoner?" Jacques's tone softened. "We're amazing, wonderful and more?"

"Yes, Sir," he answered aloud, remembering that his thoughts were being broadcast to them.

"So are you, babe," Jacques said with a tenderness that shocked him. "Ready?"

"Yes, Sir." He bit the sheets, bracing himself.

Jacques brought the paddle down to his ass, delivering a whack that caused Levi's mind to drift up and away. Surreal. The little bits of pain were taken him higher, away from his guilt.

"Seven, Sir. Commander. Eight. Nine. Ten, Sir. Commander."

He was both in his body and out of it. He felt like he was looking into eternity—his eternity with his immortals.

He continued the counting as Jacques carried out his punishment to his backside. The stings were only slightly more than Reno had provided earlier. Still, they were enough to keep his mind floating in bliss. The final one came down, a bit less than the previous ones had been.

"Seventeen, Sir. Commander." His entire body hummed like a jet, readying for takeoff.

Jacques leaned down. Now, they were face to face.

He cupped his chin. "You did great, Levi."

"Thank you, Sir."

Jacques's lips skimmed over his mouth, sending him even higher than before.

"Reno, I want to fill up his hot ass, tonight."

"That's perfect, since I want to feel him inside me again."

"Excellent." Jacques rolled Levi onto his side to face Reno.

Levi could feel Jacques spread his ass cheeks wide. When Jacques dove into him with his tongue while Reno stroked his cock up and down with his hand, the pressure inside him pushed him to the very edge of sanity. Their handling of his body thrilled him. For the first time in his life, he felt like he really belonged, not to the Conclave, but to Jacques and Reno.

Jacques grabbed the bottle of lubricant that Reno had conjured earlier. Levi heard the plastic container's lid pop loudly. Then, he felt Jacques apply its slick contents to his backside entrance. One of Jacques's fingers entered him, stretching the tight ring.

Levi tensed.

"Relax," Jacques whispered in his ear. "You're doing great, my sweet prisoner."

My sweet prisoner. Oh God, yes!

Another finger. In and out. The more Jacques drilled into him with his digits, the more he wanted.

God, I need his dick inside me.

Jacques sent, *That's what I need from you, too, Levi,* my cock *inside you.*

"Yes, Sir. Please."

Jacques pulled him down the bed until his hips were half-on and half-off the mattress. Standing behind him, Jacques held onto his thighs so his legs and feet remained off the bed and floor.

"Breathe, prisoner," Jacques commanded.

"Yes, Sir."

Jacques slid slowly inside him, filling him utterly and completely.

Levi closed his eyes tight, feeling the wonderful pressure. "Oh God, yes. Yes." All resistance in his body vanished, leaving only hot, silky want. *How can I hold back my orgasm?*

"You will. You must." The softness he'd heard earlier in Jacques's tone had gone. Now, he sounded demanding and *hungry!*

As Jacques increased his pace in and out of his backside,

Reno growled, "Fucking unbelievable. You both look so hot."

In a flash, Jacques pulled out of him and flipped him around face up. Now with his back to the mattress, Levi lifted his legs up and over his lover's shoulders.

Jacques grinned wickedly and plunged into him again.

Closing his eyes at the incredible pleasure, Levi wiggled his hips, hoping to drive him even wilder. It must've worked as he heard him groaning like a beast delivering new, lusty strokes inside him with more intensity and speed.

"Open your eyes, babe." Jacques commanded.

"Yes, Sir." Levi complied and stared into Jacques's intense gray eyes.

Jacques smiled. "Ready to come?"

"Yes, Sir but—" Levi stopped. Jacques hadn't asked him to elaborate.

"Go on," he instructed.

"If I come now it won't be tripling."

"You're correct, it isn't." He chuckled. "Still, I'm adding five more to your paddling count for your insubordination. Understand?"

"Yes, Sir."

"Jacques, slow down," Reno said. "I want to triple."

"I know," Jacques answered. "But I can't hold back much longer."

Together, they rolled Levi on his side and then on top of Jacques, his cock remaining inside him. Jacques's muscled body cradled his back, and his hands slid down his sides.

"Fuck, yeah!" Reno smiled down at him. "That hot dick you got, sweetheart, is so inviting."

Reno leaned in and licked up and down his shaft.

Levi felt his balls get heavy and his cock jerk when Reno swallowed him whole. He felt his pulse burning his veins. When Reno swirled his tongue over the tip of his dick, Levi almost gave into his pending orgasm. *Almost.*

Don't do it. Not yet. Jacques sent.

Reno slicked up his own ass and then turned around, crouching over his dick.

Levi could feel a thin layer of pleasure sweat popping up on his skin. *Please, Commander! I need to feel you.*

Reno lunged down on him, taking his dick into his tight ass, sending a ricochet of hot want throughout Levi's body.

Jacques pressed his mouth to the back of Levi's neck. It wasn't a sweet embrace, but a possessive, commanding clasp.

Levi's body lurched from where Jacques's cock pierced him to where his dick thrust into Reno.

Jacques held his waist, plowing into him like a wild man.

"Fuck me, Levi," Reno commanded. "Fuck me like you mean it."

"Yes, Commander." He plunged his dick into his immortal lover again and again. In and out. Over and over. Taking him higher and higher.

Silver light and gray smoke appeared. Then he saw red light skating outward from his body. Silver, gray, and red coalesced together. The colors blended, changed. Grew brighter.

He used his inner muscles to clamp down on to Jacques's cock and slammed as hard as he could into Reno's ass. He wanted to please his immortals as much as they had pleased him.

"You close, guys?" Reno panted out. "God, I am."

His words aroused Levi even more. Feeling their synced rhythm, remembering his delicious punishment, pushed him so close to orgasm.

"Hold on, shade. I'm close," Jacques answered.

"So am I, Sir. Commander."

"Not yet, my prisoner." Jacques breathed heavily, nipping his ear. "Not yet."

A moan slipped past Levi's lips. He shot his arms around Reno's waist so he could hold on for dear life as his orgasm inched forward inside him.

More strokes. Faster. Deeper. His body buzzed with a million sensations.

"Levi, you belong to us." Jacques's tone had softened once again, but his drilling in him didn't. "You know that, babe? Right?"

"Yes, Sir." On the edge of losing it, he prayed Jacques would let him orgasm.

"Then come for us, babe. Let go and feel the release."

"Yesss, Sir. Commander." His climax rocked him like a Cat-Five hurricane. He shot everything inside him into Reno. His rainbow vibrated in his mind.

"*Fucking A!*" Reno yelled, sending his load across his body and over his shoulder onto Levi's face.

Jacques plowed one last time into him, blasting his liquid deep into Levi's ass.

Levi closed his eyes, feeling every cell inside his body settle back into sweet exhaustion. His immortals were locked together with him, body, mind, and heart, into a Perfect Triad. Nothing could spoil that.

An explosion inside the cavern jolted Levi away from the bliss of afterglow.

"Well, well, well. What do you we have here?" Feandan's voice echoed off the stony walls.

CHAPTER 12

JACQUES FELT fury roll through him, but he couldn't move. Not even an inch. "I'll kill you, Feandan, you motherfucker."

"I don't think so. Have you already forgotten what spells I'm capable of performing?"

A portal to Jacques's old cell floated next to the bastard and the ten Conclave guardians he'd brought with him.

"How did you get a portal here? You've never been here before."

"True. But the Conclave keeps good records. I found a very old document describing your capture in full detail, including where you'd been found. I guessed that would be your hideout. So, by narrowing it down to that, a simple location spell to get a fix on you was easy. Then, the portal."

Arrogant prick. Jacques imagined squeezing the life out of him with his bare hands.

Reno's thought shot to him. *Jacques, I can't move, either. Levi, what about you?*

He trembled next him. *A little.*

"Hello, traitor." Feandan glared at Levi. "I can't wait to

chop you up into little tiny chunks and drop your remains in the ocean for the sharks to feed on. But I will take my time. I think I'll start with your toes the first day."

A protective rage multiplied inside Jacques. He used it to increase his focus on his silver sphere of power. Feandan knew they'd tripled but couldn't be aware that they were a megaton Perfect Triad bomb. Perhaps that would give him and Reno the advantage. It had to. He couldn't let Feandan torture Levi. He knew too well what horrors the Conclave could meet out, and this smug bastard was one of its most prolific experts.

"Execute me if you want, but don't torture them." Levi's voice didn't falter. "The escape was my doing, not theirs."

"Where's *my* book?" Feandan's face darkened. "Tell me that, and I might make your death swift."

Reno, can you access your power? Jacques sent out.

I think I can, Reno answered silently.

He directed a thought to Levi. *You have your rainbow. You know how to use it?*

Not really, Levi sent back.

Try.

Yes, Sir.

"Well?" Feandan demanded. "My book?"

When the bastard jerked Levi off the bed by his hair, Jacques couldn't wait any longer. With his mind he grabbed the power from his swirling sphere and sent it flying at Feandan and the guards. Out of the corner of his eye he watched Reno fire his gray smoky ball at them, too.

All but Feandan and two others fell on the ground in pain. Those who had fallen screamed and then went silent.

Suddenly, Jacques could feel the paralysis of Feandan's spell melt away. Now that he could move, Jacques leapt from the bed, knocking Feandan to the ground with a loud thud. Reno also attacked, punching the bastard's remaining two conscious companions and knocking them out.

Before Jacques could react, Feandan glared at him. "*Yak-lisak-blusto-wan-wan-wan...*"

Jacques had no power to counteract the fucker's spell, but that didn't mean he couldn't kill him with his bare hands.

As he landed a last punch to Feandan's mouth, sending several teeth flying across the floor, the bastard shouted the last syllable of his spell.

Jacques felt a giant ball of pain in the middle of his chest that doubled him over. By the sound he could hear coming from Reno, he knew that his friend also suffered from the Feandan's dark magic.

"Jacques? Reno?" Levi's words were filled with fear. "Are you all right?"

Jacques tried to choke out an answer for him, but all he could produce was incomprehensible grunts.

Plus, Feandan's pain spell continued to grow inside him like an exploding nova.

Blast him with that rainbow power of yours, Jacques sent to Levi.

I've tried but it's not working. He shot back. "Release them, Feandan," Levi shouted aloud. "And I'll show you where the book is hidden."

"No deal, traitor." Standing alone, Feandan stepped back from Levi, clearly terrified. He was a coward but a powerful coward, who was starting another spell. "Aken esten belen..."

Jacques could see Feandan's spell starting to gather a ball of dark energy in front of him.

Try this, Reno sent out silently. *Damn, this shit hurts.*

Try what, shade? Jacques shot back, fighting against Feandan's pain spell.

Levi, try to send your rainbow power into Jacques and me.

Could that really work? Levi shot back.

Who knows, but it's got to be worth a try.

Do it. Send us your power. It's our only hope.

He watched Levi's eyes close.

"You've got to be kidding me," Feandan said, stopping his incantation, causing the dark energy's vibration to slow.

Jacques saw that the bastard's arrogance gave them a little more time for Levi to figure out Reno's plan. He sent a thought to Reno. *Let's keep him talking.*

Reno nodded. "So, you're afraid of Levi's magic?"

Feandan glared at the shade. "I'm the First of the Conclave. I know more spells than you can even dream of, monster." Feandan turned back to Levi, spreading his arms wide in a clear sign of a condescending invitation. "Send me your best shot, traitor. I'll turn it on you so fast you won't even know what hit you." Feandan once again began mumbling an ancient bloodline spell. "*Disos-Comek-Parnle.*" Must've been a big one since his chants went on and on and the dark energy began to multiply.

"Feandan, that doesn't sound right to me," Jacques mocked. "You sure you're getting it right?"

"Shut up, phantom," the creep shouted. "Of course I'm getting it right."

Fighting against the increasing torture inside him, Jacques curled his fingers into fists. If Feandan finished the incantation, all hell would break loose and Levi would be dead.

Together, they could stop him, but they had to act now.

Jacques sent, *Believe in yourself, Levi. You have the power. Use it.*

I'm trying. Really I am.

I know you are, babe. No matter what happens, I want you to know that you are not to blame. Not for any of this.

Suddenly, the pain left Jacques's body and energy flowed into him like a flood. His silver sphere grew to a size that amazed him. Reno's gray smoke nearly filled the cavern.

Feandan's eyes widened, but he continued the spell, "*Rotarnel-Begso...*" The dark energy he was gathering began to pulse wildly, burning Jacques's skin.

He and Reno sent magical bombs at the fucker. The bastard wasn't able to finish his spell, and the black power that he'd amassed so far vanished into nothingness.

Jacques lurched forward. Feandan screamed and tried to jump into the portal to escape.

No luck for the bastard.

Reno knocked him to the floor and stood over him.

Feandan conjured a dagger, throwing it at Reno, who deflected it with ease.

Another dagger appeared in his hand.

Another toss.

A miss.

And another.

Then, the prick got back to his feet. He looked back and forth at Reno and him. Then he looked at Levi, and his face darkened.

"Enough!" Jacques bulldozed into Feandan, and landed on top of him while the fiend's back remained against the floor.

"Mercy, phantom!" Feandan begged. "Have mercy!"

He glance over at Reno. "What do you think, shade?"

Reno shrugged. "Your call, buddy."

Levi screamed, "Look out!"

Jacques turned back just in time to see Feandan pull out a long, deadly blade. He knocked it out of the bastard's hand. The knife sliced the side of Feandan's neck wide open.

Jacques watched his torturer's blood pour out of his wound like a flood.

CHAPTER 13

3) BLESSED IS the human who finds love in the arms of two Rogues.
The Book of Timu: Verse 3—Chapter 15

———

Levi finished up the preparations of the meal. It was his turn to cook dinner, which he loved doing for his two immortals. Tonight was special. It was their first anniversary together and he wanted it to go perfect.

The table was set, the candles lit and the food was ready.

"Where are they?" he said aloud.

He looked out the kitchen window to the expanse beyond.

Using old Rogue contacts, Jacques had been able to purchase five hundred acres in West Texas for the three of them. It was a very remote place.

Reno had been thrilled at the choice. Though he couldn't recall much of his early mortal life, he remembered that he'd worked livestock. Jacques had thought it would be a good idea to have some horses and cattle to keep up the front for any nosy locals. They had six horses and one hundred head of cattle.

Levi loved being around the animals, loved the fresh air, and especially loved the sunrises and sunsets at their little slice of paradise.

His mind drifted back to Feandan's attack. So much had happened since that fateful night. The bastard was dead. They had the Conclave's magical blade. It was clear why Feandan had brought it with him to the cavern, but instead of helping him overcome Jacques and Reno, he had suffered a fatal blow from the weapon. Reno was the one who suggested they return to Levi's room to get the book he'd hidden. Without the blade and the book, the Conclave would be without two important weapons. That was a good thing.

They had also rescued the two immortals that Feandan and the Conclave had used to replace Jacques and Reno as their source of power. The angel and jinn were grateful for being rescued but had gone their separate ways as soon as they were free.

Levi spotted Jacques and Reno riding up their dirt road to the house. They were both smiling. It must have been a good day for them. Tomorrow, Levi would ride out with Reno and Jacques would be their cook, which likely meant hamburgers or spaghetti for dinner being the only two things Jacques could whip up.

Levi turned his attention back to getting the plates of food on the table, since his guys were about to walk in the door.

He suspected Jacques liked ranching more than he ever admitted to him and Reno. Jacques was known to use any excuse to saddle up his horse to check on the fences, or a well, or the herd at the drop of a hat.

He heard the door open in the other room.

"Is that fried chicken I smell?" Jacques asked. "Our little prisoner knows just how to please us, doesn't he Reno?"

"He sure does." Reno answered. "I smell apple pie, too. Where are you, sweetheart?"

"I'm in the kitchen, Commander."

Jacques laughed and said, "Get in here, babe."

"Yes, Sir."

Levi entered the living room. As always, the sight of them thrilled him. They looked so sexy in their cowboy hats, western shirts, tight jeans, and dusty boots.

"Damn, you two look good enough to eat," he confessed.

"As do you, babe," Jacques said, pulling him in for a kiss.

Reno wrapped his arms around the both of them. "Is there anything better than the three of us?"

"Not a chance." Levi trembled with desire for the two immortals that had changed everything for the better for him. "I live to serve you, Commander. Sir."

There was a long pause as they all took in the moment.

Jacques spoke first. "Look at me, my sweet prisoner."

He obeyed.

Jacques's gaze was warm. "You're the best thing that ever happened to me."

"Same for me, Sir. Happy anniversary."

Jacques kissed him deeply. "I love you, Levi."

Levi felt sparks shoot through him hearing those words from Jacques for the first time.

"I love you, too, sweetheart." Reno came up behind Levi and started rubbing his shoulders. "And if the truth be known, I love this old grumpy pants phantom, too."

"Grumpy pants? Really?" Jacques grinned. "I love you too, shade, but don't ever call me that again."

Reno laughed. "We'll see."

"God, I love you both so very much," Levi confessed.

Jacques cupped his chin. "I couldn't be happier."

Reno kissed the back of Levi's neck. "Me either, buddy. Me either."

"Are you guys hungry?" Levi grinned, reaching out and placing a hand on each of their crotches through the denim.

They were already hard. An expectant electric shock shot through him, and his cock began to lengthen.

"Naughty prisoner." Jacques grinned. "I think you should be punished."

"Yes, Sir."

"I like this idea," Reno said, running his hand up and down Levi's arm. "Dinner can wait, right, sweetheart?"

"Yes, Commander. Dinner can wait. I'm hungry for something much more satisfying. But you two need to shower first."

"You want to scrub us clean, babe?" Jacques asked, kissing Levi.

"Yes, Sir. Please."

His two immortals carried him back into the bathroom, caressing him along the way.

Eternity would be just perfect with his two Rogues.

THE END

ABOUT THE AUTHOR

Lee Swift, who writes under several pen names including Kris Cook, creates novels, short stories, screenplays and more.

With an unquenchable thirst to experience all his life journey has to offer, Lee and hubby love travel but still call Dallas, Texas home.

Join [HERE] to get updates on Lee.

ALSO BY LEE SWIFT

Novels

Morvicti Blood *(Supernatural Thriller)*

Cupid's Arrow *(Gay Fantasy Romance)*

Three to Play *(Menage MMF Romance)*

(All series listed in best reading order)

Mockingbird Place

(Gay Romance Series)

The Marine in Unit A

The Cowboy in Unit E

The Fireman in Unit C

The Doctor in Unit H

The Fighter in Unit J

Holiday Beaus (Novella)

The Musician in Unit G

The Cop in Unit B

Wolf Pack

(Menage MFM Romance Trilogy)

Secret Cravings

Primal Desires

Delicious Hunger

Eternal Trio Series

(Gay Menage Fantasy Romance)

Levi's Rogues

Perfection

Writing with Lana Lynn

(Thrillers)

Lexi's Protector *(Men Without A Cause)*

Liz's Guardian *(Men Without A Cause)*

Secret Diary Series as Kris Cook

(Erotic Straight BDSM Trilogy)

Mia's Spanking Diary

Misty's Bondage Diary

Lea's Ménage Diary